I0760722

THE LUCKY ONES

KIERSTEN MODGLIN

Copyright © 2020 by Kiersten Modglin
All rights reserved.
No part of this book may be reproduced in any form or by any electronic or mechanical means, including information storage and retrieval systems, without written permission from the author, except for the use of brief quotations in a book review.
This is a work of fiction. Names, characters, places, and incidents are either the product of the author's imagination or are used fictitiously. Any resemblance to locales, events, business establishments, or actual persons—living or dead—is entirely coincidental.

www.kierstenmodglinauthor.com
Cover Design: Tadpole Designs
Editing: Three Owls Editing
Proofreading: My Brother's Editor
Formatting: Tadpole Designs
First Print Edition: 2020
First Electronic Edition: 2020

PRAISE FOR THE LUCKY ONES

This book started with a bang, and never slowed down!

Complete with her signature twists, unique plot, and suspense that keeps you turning the pages, Modglin's The Lucky Ones is a book not to be missed!

EMERALD O'BRIEN, AUTHOR OF THE KNOX AND SHEPPARD MYSTERY SERIES

No one does twists better than [Modglin.]

CHRISTINE, GOODREADS REVIEWER

Watch out for Kiersten Modglin! This author is ridiculously talented and provides a smooth, seamless story with engaging characters and a plot that keeps you turning the pages,

BOOKS AND COFFEE BLOG

"...another suspenseful, haunting and amazing book from Kiersten Modglin [with] a shocking and surprising ending that you will never forget."

LISA, GOODREADS REVIEWER

To my 4 Authors and a Mystery sisters—
For being the ones I go to when I need a friend.

CHAPTER ONE

October 5th

They came for us in the night. Like vandals, they broke into our houses. The noise of their intrusion tore us from our beds. I remember wondering what was happening. In my half-asleep state, none of it made any sense. Who were these strangers? Why were they there? What did they want? My teenage mind couldn't comprehend the horror that was beginning to unfold.

I stumbled from my bed, awakened by my mother's screams coming from my parents' bedroom. I couldn't hear my dad. Where was he? Why wasn't he helping her? Deep down, I already knew.

As I walked down the hall, barefoot and dressed in pajamas, I saw a masked man sauntering through my house as if it were his own. He made his way down the hall, barely missing me as I hurried to hide beside a bookcase in the alcove, and joined another man in my parents' bedroom. Would they come for me next? What was I supposed to do?

Panic immediately set in, wiping the last trace of sleep from my mind as I realized we were truly in danger. My sister and I. My parents. I had no weapons—no means to protect us against our enemies. As I heard a third set of footsteps coming up the stairs, I darted into my sister's bedroom. She was huddled under the covers, a lump of pink and white, shivering and crying as she awaited her fate. Even at seven years old, she was old enough to recognize danger.

"Cassie, are you okay?" I asked, pulling the covers from her head. Tears trailed down her cheeks as she looked up at me. As recognition flooded her face, she lunged at me, throwing her arms around my neck.

"Ellie, what's going on?" she asked, her tiny voice quivering.

"There are people in the house," I told her, keeping my voice low. I looked to her window. We were on the second story, but we weren't going to survive going out into the hallway again, and we may not survive staying in this room for much longer. The window was our only option.

"Are they hurting Mom?" she whimpered.

I placed a careful hand around her head. "I need to get you out of here. Mom will be fine," I assured her, though I wasn't at all sure myself. Her screams could still be heard from her bedroom. I wanted nothing more than to rush to her, but I couldn't. I knew my job was to protect my little sister. I brushed away tears as quickly as they fell, refusing to give in to the fear that filled my belly.

I stood from the bed, walking to the window and pushing it open. I looked out in horror at what had become of my street since I saw it last. Everywhere I looked, my neighbors ran wild. Bodies lay dead in their yards. I heard gunshots ringing out from another house, followed by more screams.

Another man in a mask gunned down the woman from across the street in her yard. She froze, her hands in the air as she begged him not to shoot. I looked away, wincing as I heard the shot. The bodies were all dressed in pajamas. No one had been prepared. We hadn't seen them coming.

Fear seized my organs, and I contemplated crawling into a closet and hoping they'd miss us. Who could say if going out was any safer than staying in? When I heard a gunshot down the hall, I yelped in surprise. My heart thudded in my chest so loudly I could hear nothing else.

"What was that?" she asked, though I knew she had to know.

I reached out, taking hold of her hand. "Come on, Cass. We need to move. Now."

"Out the window?" she asked, fear in her voice. "We can't!"

"Shhh!" I shushed her as she grew too loud. It was too late. I'd known it from the moment she squealed. Heavy footsteps headed our direction instantly. I scooped her from the bed without warning, pushing her out the window and onto the roof. She took cautious steps across the shingles, looking back to me for guidance.

As her bedroom door flew open, an unrecognizable stranger in her doorway, I pushed myself out behind her, rushing toward the edge. I looked down, staring at the grass as I counted to three in my head.

"It's too far," Cassie cried, shaking her head and pulling away from me. I looked over my shoulder as the man climbed out on the roof. Without choice, I held my sister in my arms, launching us off the roof and onto the grass.

It was harder than I expected. As I landed, my feet were knocked out from under me and we both slammed into the ground. I coughed, the wind knocked out of me, as I leaned over and reached for my sister. She sat up, tears still in her eyes, as she attempted to catch her breath from the fall. She clutched her chest, speaking through heavy breaths. "Where are Mom and Dad?" she asked, her voice full of despair. I couldn't answer, but based on the expression on her face, I didn't need to. I looked across the street, where my neighbors lay slaughtered in their yards.

"Ellie!" a voice called behind me. I looked up to see Gray MacTavish, a teenage boy around my age with wild red hair and blue eyes, running toward me. He reached out a hand. "Come on." I let him lift me from the ground, my head still fuzzy from the fall. I helped my sister to her feet and followed Gray as he led us toward the woods behind our neighborhood. We darted around a car that flew down the dead-end street. More gunfire rang out in the distance, only slightly drowned out by the screams.

That's what I remember most. Screaming. Everyone was screaming. And for good reason. As we darted into the woods, we met a few others—kids we barely knew, who would quickly become like family. Because soon enough, they'd be all we had left. The next day, when the murderers had disappeared and we were strong enough to be able to make our way back into our subdivision, we walked over the bodies of the people we'd loved with a new callousness in our hearts. We weren't the children we'd been the day before. Our innocence, our belief in the good in people, had been taken right out from under us. There was no going back.

We'd been prepared for it, we thought. We knew what to do in a crisis. School had prepared us for active shooters and bombs, earthquakes and tornadoes. But how could anyone prepare for something like this?

There were only a handful of men, but they'd done irreparable damage in record time. In the months and years to come, people would try to piece together exactly what happened and why. They'd try to make sense of a senseless crime. To everyone who heard, it was a tragic end to so many lives, but eventually it was forgotten and we were all that was left. Somehow, the five of us, just kids at the time, had made it out. We were lucky, so they said. We'd survived.

I don't know, maybe I'm cynical. It never felt like surviving to me.

CHAPTER TWO

October 2nd
Five Years Later

"We're coming up on the anniversary," my therapist said casually, crossing one tweed-covered leg over the other. *Anniversary.* As if it were something to be celebrated. As if a party were in order. I glared at him harder, his beady eyes set too far apart behind thick glasses.

"Mhm," I said and squeezed my hands together in my lap. No doubt he'd notice that and make a record of it somewhere in his notes. What he did with those notes, I'd never been allowed to know.

"How are you feeling about that?" he asked, his gray mustache twitching. Was that really what he wanted to know? I could really freak him out with a positive answer, I supposed, but instead, I shrugged.

"I don't know. Trying not to think about it, I guess." I chewed on a bit of loose skin around my forefinger.

"How about Cassie? How is she handling it?"

I thought about my sister then, the nervous twelve-year-old who still jumped when something was dropped near her. The rest of the survivors: myself, Gray, Cole, and Monica, were all teenagers when it happened. Practically adults. Cassie was the youngest survivor and the one who seemed to deal with the most anxiety over it all. Not that any of us had handled it particularly well.

"Same as always. She's not okay, but she's never okay."

He wrote something else down in his journal, and I stared out the window, feeling the cool air from the ceiling fan hit me. I rubbed my arm, trying to warm up in the chilly environment where I'd spent every Tuesday evening for the past four years of my life. The first year after it happened I was a mess. I was *still* a mess, truth be told, but now I just spent money to hear about it.

"Have you been journaling?" he asked, jumping straight from the subject of my sister to my homework as if he were marking things off a checklist. Maybe he was.

"Mhm." Doctor Porter said the journaling was for me. So I could keep an accurate account of where I was emotionally related to everything going on around me. He wanted me to have somewhere I could be completely honest, even more so than he thought I could be with him. He told me he'd never ask to see the journal, that he just wanted to know I was doing it.

How could I know, though? How could I trust him? I couldn't, that's the answer. I couldn't trust him because I couldn't trust anyone.

So, sure, I filled out the journal nightly, but I filled it with half-truths. I wrote about how much I disliked the color red, but I didn't mention that I disliked it because every time I saw it, all I could think about was the way the black pavement had been painted red with blood that morning. I wrote about how I got overwhelmed in a crowd that day, but I didn't mention how I pictured just how easy it would be to pull a knife and slice into the kidneys of the man standing in front of me. I wrote about how I felt about getting passed up for a promotion at work again. I didn't mention that when I was walking to my car with the girl who'd gotten the promotion, I thought about how I would escape if I were to stick the letter opener from my desk into her throat. How hard I'd have to scrub to get the blood out of my clothes. Whether there were cameras around that would catch my crime. Half-truths. Compromise. I painted the picture he and the rest of the world wanted to see. The girl whose tragic past had made her a victim. The girl who watched an entire subdivision of people get slaughtered at sixteen years old. I didn't tell them the truth because no one could handle it. The truth was, the past hadn't made me a victim like everyone thought; I think it made me a monster.

CHAPTER THREE

October 2nd

I walked across the damp sidewalk that led to my apartment, my arms wrapped around me to keep me warm in the brisk, fall air. If someone were listening, they could've heard me coming. They'd hear my footsteps on the wet concrete, notice the way my jeans scraped the ground. If someone wanted to, they could've hidden in wait until I was too close to run. They could've gotten me if they wanted.

Those thoughts flooded my mind with my every waking moment. I knew how easily accessible I was. How easily accessible we all were. We may try to hide behind false security, but the truth is, none of us are safe.

I pulled the key from my jacket pocket and stuck it into the lock, turning it quickly. With a glance over my shoulder, I pushed the door open and dashed inside. I locked it behind me before I could let out a breath.

Safety. The feeling washed over me. Although I knew I was still not completely guarded behind my two deadbolts, this was the safest place I knew. The safest place I'd known in five years.

I walked over toward the window and lifted the blind with one finger. Few cars were in the parking lot at that hour; most people were still at work. I put the blind back down and paced the room, checking everything. I needed to know that things were still where I'd left them. That no one had invaded my home. The side door of the apartment was never unlocked, but I checked it anyway, pulling on the door handle for good measure. The screws that held the hinges in place were extra long, tough enough to stall even the strongest intruder. The small patio on the other side of the door was lined with aluminum cans. To my neighbors, I looked like a slob, but I knew the truth. If someone jumped over the bushes that hid the green railing to my porch, they'd land on the cans. If they made enough noise, I hoped they'd get scared and run away. If not, I'd at least have enough of a warning to get out the front door. I'd counted the steps in between the front and side doors incessantly. Forty-seven. I knew either escape route from my apartment backward and forward, in the light or in the dark. I could get out if I needed to. I'd made sure of it.

I ran my fingers across the desk and bookshelves, across the back of my chair. I walked carefully toward the bedroom, checking that my bed was still made, that my clothes remained on their hangers. No one had done anything. No one had been there.

Finally, I pushed out an exaggerated breath of relief that let me know I was home. I pulled the jacket from my arms, shaking off the excess water from the rain, and hung it up on the rack beside the front door.

I turned around, walked into the kitchen, and filled the

kettle with water before placing it on the stove. I stood in front of the stove, watching the burner grow orange with heat, and I contemplated placing my hand on the heat. What would I feel? Would it hurt worse than I could even fathom? Those were the thoughts that haunted me. Was that normal? Thoughts about hurting people…and myself. I wasn't depressed, as far as I knew. It wasn't like I wanted to act on them, it just…fascinated me, I guess. The realization of how close we all were to evil. To danger. To death. I didn't remember thinking about that before I turned sixteen, before that terrible morning, but the thoughts were always there now. Waiting. Watching. Listening for their in.

As a knock sounded on my door, causing me to jump, I turned my head quickly. Standing frozen in panic, my throat tight and my blood running icy through my veins, I waited. I counted, breathing slowly as if they could hear my breaths through the door.

After several minutes had passed, I walked toward the door, thankful I still had my shoes on. Truth be told, I had no idea why that mattered. But there was that thought: *at least I still have my shoes on.* I reached for the door handle as if it were the scorching burner from the stove—slow and with a shaking hand. I pictured the men's faces again, the black ski masks that I would never forget. What if they'd come back for me? I pulled the duct tape off the peephole and glanced outside. No one was there. At least, no one was in my line of vision. I leaned one way and then the other, trying to make sure there was no one waiting for me.

With no other option, I placed a hand on the lock, resting my entire body against the white door as I sucked in a deep breath, letting it out slowly as I'd been taught to do when I felt a panic attack coming on. I waited until I could wait no longer, turning the cold metal of the knob in my hand.

I had my eyes closed as I pulled open the door, though I had no idea why that was. In hindsight, it was the worst way to react to such a situation. When I opened them—slowly and one at a time—I breathed heavily.

My view through the peephole had been correct. There was no one in my doorway. No masked man, no Girl Scout selling cookies. I looked down the long breezeway, searching for the source of the sound. Had I imagined it? Perhaps someone was knocking on a different door. Surely I'd heard it. About to give up, I moved back, gasping suddenly as my eyes landed on what awaited me.

On the dingy, brown welcome mat, lay a crisp, white envelope. There was no writing on the outside. As I picked it up, two white daisies fell out of the top, landing in my hand. They'd been crushed by the paper, their petals wilted. I had a sickening feeling filling my belly as I closed the door and flipped both deadbolts. Everything in me told me to throw the letter away, toss it aside without reading it and never think about it again. But I couldn't. The sick, paranoid part of my brain had to know. I turned it over, looking at the unsealed part. What secrets did this letter hold?

I stared at it, blinking endlessly as my mind twisted and turned with every dreadful scenario—human teeth, fingernails, a court summons, photographs of myself taken by a stalker, death threats. As I finally reached for the paper, willing myself to stop thinking and just read it, my hands shook. I pulled the paper out. No teeth fell to the floor. I turned the paper over in my hands, sliding my finger in between the fold to read it.

SCREEEECH! The kettle screamed from across the room,

causing me to throw the paper, and my heart nearly leaping from my throat. I cursed loudly, hurrying toward the stove and grabbing a potholder to move it from the burner as I turned it off. I shook my head, running a hand over my forehead in exasperation. As I turned back around, looking for the paper I'd lost, my jaw dropped. It lay open on the floor, the words that will haunt me for the rest of my life lying open on full display.

Two little daisies, ready to pluck.
We're coming for you, daisies, don't count on your luck.

CHAPTER FOUR

October 2nd

I paced my living room, *back and forth, back and forth,* the flip phone in one hand, paper in the other. I stared at Gray's number, a number I never planned to use when he gave it to me on Thanksgiving a few years ago. I had no idea if he even still used it, truth be told, but it was a shot I had to take.

"Hello?" His carefree voice rang out over the line.

"Gray?" I glanced across the room to where the clock showed it was just past three. Cassie would be getting home from school soon, and I didn't want her to hear the conversation I was about to have. "Er, Gray McTavish?"

"Speaking," he said, clearing his throat. "Who is this?"

"Gray, it's Ellie."

"Ellie?" he asked, going silent for a moment before I heard him suck in a breath. "Ellie Delanoe?"

"Yes," I said. It made me nervous, speaking to him again. Truth be told, I didn't like using the phone at all. I'd refused to get one for the longest time, but when I was granted guardianship of Cassie just after my eighteenth birthday, the school requested that I have a cell phone in case of an emergency. I gave in, in the form of a flip phone with no internet access. There were too many ways for people to find you on the internet. Too much danger. In the end, they'd found me anyway.

"Whoa, okay. Um, how are you?" His voice was slow and deep, allowing for plenty of time to process. I shook my head, wondering just what his life had become since I'd last seen him. When we'd parted ways before, I'd never wanted to see any of the *Fallen Oaks Five,* as we'd been dubbed, again.

"Not good. Listen, did you get a letter?" I blurted out, staring at my own letter where it still remained on the carpet. I had no desire to touch it, and I was pretty sure that when I had to, I was going to stab it with a knife and throw it away, knife and all.

"What kind of letter?" he asked. His tone told me all that I needed to know. He wasn't scared. He hadn't received the same warning I had. Not yet, anyway.

"I got a letter today." It was all that I could muster, but I knew it wouldn't be enough. I had to elaborate, though I desperately didn't want to.

"A letter? Is everything okay?"

"It was from...*them.*" I forced the words out, unaware that cool tears had formed in my eyes until my vision began to blur. I wiped them away quickly, though no one could see them in the sanctuary of my own home.

"Them?" His happy voice suddenly grew very serious, and I knew he knew what I meant. I didn't have to say any more for him to grasp my words. It was a truth that had haunted us all, I assumed. Wondering when our families' killers would be back. They'd never been caught. The police hadn't turned up a single suspect, and they'd widely publicized the fact that we survived. Though we were minors and they were never allowed to publish our photos or names, I knew it would be easy enough to find out who the survivors were. There were only five of us, after all. In truth, I was surprised they hadn't tracked us down sooner.

"Yes," I answered his question finally. "There were two daisies. It said they are coming for us."

He was silent, the only sign that he remained on the line was his deep breathing. "Is it addressed to you?"

"No," I answered, though the question seemed silly. "It was left in front of my door, though."

"So, you don't know for sure it's for you, right?"

"Who else would it be for, Gray?" My agitation with him was growing as I watched the minutes on the clock tick by. Any minute now, Cassie would be getting off the bus. Suddenly, the thought struck me and fear grabbed my heart. *Cassie.* I couldn't leave her to get off the bus alone with the possibility that the person who'd left my note was still out there.

"I mean, I don't know, I'm just…I'm just saying don't be paranoid, okay?"

I groaned, rushing toward the door. "I have to go, Gray."

"Don't be mad," he warned.

"I have to go," I said again, flipping my phone shut as I pulled the door shut and locked it behind me while keeping a careful watch over my shoulder as I did. I wouldn't be gone long, but I wouldn't dare chance leaving the door unlocked. Not even for a second.

I made a mad dash down the breezeway, the dampness of the sidewalk sloshing under my feet. I looked all around, watching to see if anyone was paying special attention to me. I had to be on guard now more than ever.

As I reached the edge of the apartment complex, I spied the bus pulling up with remarkable timing. I slowed down, bending over my knees to catch my breath. I looked up, mouth open as I attempted to replenish my oxygen supply. Cassie stepped off the bus, tossing a careful wave over her shoulder to someone behind her. When she spied me, her face went ashen. She rushed toward me as I stood up straight.

"What's wrong?" she demanded. She knew me so well.

"Come inside," I instructed, taking hold of her shoulder and hurrying back to the safety of our apartment. Once we were back inside, she stared at me, her brow raised.

"Is everything okay?"

"I don't think it is, Cassie." I didn't want to tell her. I didn't want to burden her with all that worried me, but what choice did I have? Cassie had been forced to grow up so long ago, and though I'd attempted to give her some semblance of a normal life, we both knew that was no longer possible. Not when you've held your parents' lifeless bodies in your arms. Not when you've tracked their blood across the carpet where you once played with Barbies. "I think we're in danger."

She swallowed, waiting for me to go on. I bent down, picking up the letter finally and turning it over in my hand. The daisies lay on the carpet still. She read it carefully, her eyes darting across the page.

"What does it mean, Ellie?" she asked, her voice shaking.

"It could be a prank," I offered, though we both knew that wasn't the case.

"How did they find us?" she asked. Her lips began to

quiver, her dark eyes hidden behind strands of honey-brown hair filling with tears.

"It's going to be okay." I made her a promise we both knew I couldn't keep. "We're going to call the police. Show them this letter. We'll be safe this time, Cassie."

She sniffled, rubbing a thumb under her nose. My heart ached for her, and for myself, too. What had we done to deserve such a fate? That was a selfish thing to wonder, I supposed, but I wondered anyway. She reached forward, taking the paper from my hand. "Where was this?" she asked, her brow furrowing.

I pointed toward the door as the smell of tea began to permeate the air. I'd almost forgotten about the tea I'd put on earlier. "It was left on the door—" I stopped as my phone's ring cut me off. We both stared at each other, our eyes wide with fear. As I slipped the phone out of my pants pocket, I let out a breath. "It's okay. It's Gray."

"Gray? From—"

"Yes." I opened the phone, placing it to my ear. "Hello?"

"Ellie?" he said my name with a tone that sent cold chills across my body. I watched as the hair on my arms stood on end, and Cassie seemed to sense that something was wrong by the way she was staring at me. She leaned forward in an attempt to hear the conversation. I pulled it out, looking for the button to turn it on speakerphone, but before I'd accomplished that, he spoke again. With my volume up, we heard his words clearly anyway, though sometimes I wish we hadn't. "We all got the letters."

CHAPTER FIVE

October 2nd

Eight hours later, the survivors—people who were still practically strangers to me despite all we'd gone through together—gathered in my living room. I looked between them, faces that had not aged well, eyes that were weighed down with the horrors of the things we'd seen. The worry of what we were about to be dealing with plagued us all, and we found ourselves, once again, facing the world... alone, yet together.

The first to speak was Cole, and I believe that took no one by surprise. The former quarterback of our high school, a rich boy who was set to go to an Ivy League school had fate not had other ideas, Cole had always been the natural leader of our accidental group.

"So, everyone got the same letter? And they all arrived today?" We all nodded, each of us clutching the letters in our hands. It was unbelievable, we knew that. None of us had stayed anywhere near Fallen Oaks, and we all lived miles and states apart. How had they found all of us? It wasn't possible. How had anyone managed to pull off something so grand in just a few hours? It made no logical sense. It would've taken at least four people to track down each of us and plant the letters simultaneously. As much as I wanted to believe it was a prank, that someone was only toying with us because of the impending anniversary, I knew that couldn't be the case. Which only left the improbable, albeit undeniable, truth…the men who had killed our families, the group that had planned their deaths, was back…and they were coming for us next. I wrung my hands together at the thought, chewing on my bottom lip with worry. Anxiety filled me, fear of what was coming, and fear of who'd been in my doorway. Were they watching the apartment right then? I couldn't be sure.

"What do we do?" Monica, a small, mousy girl who'd only gotten smaller and more quiet with age, asked. She wrapped her frail arms around herself as if she were cold, though my apartment, with three extra bodies filling it, was anything but chilly. I couldn't bear to think of the answer to her question. It hurt too much. Scared me too much.

"I say we call the police," Gray answered, looking to Cole for support. Gray had always been first to agree with Cole in school, though Cole rarely reciprocated. Gray rested on the arm of my couch, looking far more casual than any of us could've possibly been feeling.

Cole seemed to think for a moment before nodding. "Yeah, okay."

I could see that the answer troubled him as much as it did me. The idea of the police coming here, intruding on the solace of my apartment, was enough to induce a panic attack. I had an inkling we all felt the same way about the men who were supposed to protect us all those years ago. My first grievance with the police was the fact that they served as a constant reminder that they were the first people we saw alive when our families had died. Every time I'd seen a police car in the past five years, the memory sprang to the front of my mind. I remembered the way I felt, utterly and entirely alone, as they pulled into the neighborhood lined with bodies that day. I remembered riding in their cars back to the station to answer their questions, the way we'd been interrogated as if we were suspects in the beginning. I remembered the way they'd accused our parents of horrible things—for what sort of good people could be deserving of such a fate? I remembered the numerous times they told us no one had been caught and that they had no leads. I remembered that they failed us.

So, the idea of calling the police back into our lives made my stomach tense. It wasn't my idea of a good Friday.

"What do we tell them?" Monica asked. "And which cops do we call? The ones here in Kansas City? Or the ones in each of our individual towns?"

"What about the ones back in Fallen Oaks?" Gray asked. "They'll know about our past. They'll understand what this all means."

"But they have no jurisdiction here," Cole argued. "Even if we tell them what's happening, they won't be able to do anything." He shook his head. "No, the smartest thing to do is for each of us to call the cops where we live. Let them handle them separately."

"But these aren't separate," I argued, surprising even myself. "You know they aren't. They're connected. This is all connected, and we have to do something before—" I cut myself off before the words slipped out, the mere thought of them enough to send tears to my eyes. They all knew what I was going to say. I could see it in each set of grief-stricken eyes.

"Before we end up just like them," Cassie finished for me from behind where I was standing. I looked over my shoulder at her, my lips tight. When she met my eyes, her gaze was firm. I nodded slightly.

"Before we end up like them," I confirmed. How was it possible that she looked so strong when we, the adults, looked so weak? My sister, who was raised in the shadow of my weakness, looked as though she were speaking of strangers, rather than our families. She was stronger than I'd ever given her credit for, and it wasn't until that moment that I fully allowed myself to realize it.

"So, what are you suggesting?" Cole asked, his gray eyes locked with mine. He still had the football player stance, all broad shoulders and thick, dark hair, and though I expected his eyes to meet mine with condescension, he genuinely looked as though he wanted an answer. As if he thought I might have a better plan than he did.

I looked across the room to where the daisies still laid on the counter, coming up with my plan on the spot. "I think we should call the cops that worked on our parents' cases. We can tell them what's happening and ask them what we should do. They will at least be able to point us in the right direction, because Monica's right," she smiled at me warmly as I spoke her praises, "even though legally, they should all probably be looked at separately—these aren't separate cases. Whoever sent us these letters, this is no coincidence. The Fallen Oaks police will at least understand the significance of all of us being targeted." I looked down at the ground as was so often my habit. I didn't believe in my plan even as I spoke it. It was stupid. Nothing made sense in that moment—not my plan, but not any of theirs either.

When Gray stood from the arm of my couch, I looked back up, half expecting them to laugh off what I'd said or tell me to leave the planning to them. Instead, he nodded, looking at Cole.

Cole's expression was serious as he nodded. "You're right," he said simply. "We should call Fallen Oaks first. Then, we'll decide what to do and where to go from there."

I stared at him, letting the words sink in. "Where to go? Figuratively or..." He couldn't possibly mean...I couldn't fathom the possibility of returning to that place. Not ever again.

"We'll figure it all out when we talk to them," he said.

"I'm not going back to Fallen Oaks," I said firmly, refusing to even call the place my home anymore. I hadn't stepped foot back in that town since that fateful day, except to attend their funeral, fuzzy as those memories were. Not even to collect my things. They were packed for me, by whom I couldn't tell you, and shipped to my grandmother's house two towns over, where Cassie and I stayed until I turned eighteen and was able to gain custody of her.

"Ellie, we'll—" Gray started to argue with me, but I cut him off instantly.

"I said I'm *not* going."

Cole held up a hand to calm the tension. "One step at a time, okay? None of us want to go back. I think we can all agree on that, right?" Without waiting for an answer from anyone, he went on. "So, we'll call the police and let them tell us what to do. There shouldn't be any reason for us to return."

I nodded, though I still wasn't totally at ease. Everything

about having these people back in my life had me on edge. They only reminded me of all that I'd lost.

"Okay, fine, so who's going to call?" Monica asked, staring around the room at each of them rather than volunteering herself. Cole was the obvious choice, so I looked at him.

"I will," he agreed halfheartedly. "How many letters do we have? Five?"

"Four," I corrected, "because Cassie and I share one. But five daisies." I held our two up, though they were beginning to wilt already.

He nodded. "Right. Okay, and they were all at your doorsteps, correct?"

We all nodded with him. It had already been discussed, but I understood his need to clarify. I would've done the same thing. Double check and then check again. It was part of my obsessive compulsive disorder, so said Doctor Porter anyway, and I wondered if Cole had the same. Mine was trauma-induced, so I supposed maybe we all had it in some form or another. Doctor Porter had told me that after experiencing trauma, the risk of compulsive behavior or a form of PTSD forming, was around thirty percent. There was a good chance it had affected us all.

"Okay," Cole said finally, glancing down at his phone as he pulled it from the pocket of his slacks. "Here we go then." He looked nervous, and I wondered if he was practicing the conversation he'd have like I so often did. I'd rehearse everything before I could make a phone call, and that was only when I was forced to make phone calls at all. When I could help it, a text was always better.

I watched as he pulled up Safari on his iPhone, searching for the phone number to Fallen Oaks Police Department. There was once a time when we all had the personal number to the detective on our case memorized, but those days had long since passed for me, and apparently for Cole, too. He clicked on the button, giving the okay for the call to begin, and placed the phone to his ear with a less-than-confident expression.

After a moment, he cleared his throat. "Yes, I'd like to speak to a detective who is familiar with the Fallen Oaks Gerbera murder case." *Gerbera*. The name of our old subdivision sent chills across my arms. He was silent, but rolled his eyes before continuing. "I know that everyone has heard of it. Do you have any detectives specifically assigned to that case? Maybe Detective Gold, if he's available." Again, he paused, his expression quickly changing to anger. "Well, it's still open, isn't it?" He nodded, though whoever was on the other line couldn't see him, and pulled the phone from his ear with a hand over the speaker. "She put me on hold."

"What's going on?" Gray asked.

"She doesn't think anyone's working that—" He lifted the phone back to his ear as we heard the woman's voice back on the line. "Yes, I'm here. Okay. Okay...okay. Thanks." Another pause. After a minute, he took a breath. "Hello, my name is Cole Dennison. I'm, um, one of the survivors of the Fallen Oaks Gerbera murders. I really need to talk to someone about the case. The five of us, er, the survivors, we...well, we think we may be in danger, and we really don't know what we should do. Anyway, please just give me a call back as soon as you get this." He left his phone number on the voicemail, repeating it twice before hanging up. "I left a voicemail for one of their lead detectives. Detective Gold retired, she said. The receptionist said if this new detective isn't heading up the case, he should know who is. It's not showing up in her database as assigned to anyone for some reason."

"Probably because Gold never cared enough to pass it off to someone," Gray said. "If you ask me, our parents never stood a chance at justice with that old asshole on the case. Couldn't even find his own daughter when she went missing, what made us think he could find the answer to anything else?" He scoffed, hatred in his voice.

I tried to ignore the fact that the phrase he'd just muttered caused my breathing to grow quicker. I had my own doubts about Gold's ability to handle our case, but could I believe that he'd be careless enough to let it slip through the cracks completely? Had they already forgotten about us? Given up on ever finding the people responsible for the murders of our families? Surely they couldn't so soon. We were still waiting for answers. Every time the phone rang, I wondered if it would be *the call.* All this time and they weren't even trying to find an answer?

"So, what do we do now?" Gray asked the question that seemed to be on everyone's mind.

Cole bit his lip, looking around my apartment. "We wait here. Together. I'll keep my phone on loud so we won't miss the call, and we'll stick together because that seems to be the safest plan." He glanced at the clock. "It's late, and I know we're all tired. Hopefully, we'll hear from the detective first thing in the morning, and then we can figure everything else out."

"So, we aren't calling the police here?" I asked. "What if we really are in danger?"

"If we don't hear back from the detective by tomorrow, we'll call the police here, but I still think your plan is the best one we've got. We have to believe that going back to Fallen Oaks is our best hope of getting this thing solved and catching the maniacs responsible for these," he gestured toward the letter in his hand, "and everything else. We owe our parents that much."

Our parents were dead, I wanted to remind him. It didn't feel like we really *owed* them anything other than surviving ourselves.

"Going back to Fallen Oaks is our best hope," I repeated his words as they rang through my mind. Somehow, that made me feel more hopeless than ever.

CHAPTER SIX

October 3rd

The next morning, I awoke before any of the others. We'd all decided to stay together in the living room, despite the fact that my bed was just a few feet away calling my name, and I'd slept next to Cassie in our oversized chair. Her cold heels dug into my sides, jarring me from sleep every few hours, so when I opened my eyes and spied the slightest hint of daylight outside, I stood from the chair, tossing the blanket over her carefully and walking to the kitchen.

I started the coffee right away. Rituals were important to me. Routine. It helped me feel more in control when I usually felt less. I liked lists and order and disliked chaos and mess. The apartment was silent, except for the odd snore, and while the coffee brewed, I slipped into the bathroom and turned on the shower. I didn't want to wake anyone up, but the urge to complete the next phase of my routine had begun to gnaw at me. As soon as I was done, I'd need to call work and Cassie's school, but that could wait until I felt clean.

I ran my hands over my hair as the scalding water fell down over my face. What revelations would the day hold? I couldn't help but think about it...wonder what would be different by the day's end. If there was one thing my life had taught me so far, it was that one day could change everything. I dumped a bit of shampoo into my palm, working it through my locks as I tried to drown out the worry, if only for a moment. There was nothing going to be solved by getting myself worked up. A panic attack under these conditions would only make things worse. I needed to be strong for Cassie—for everyone. We were in this together; if one person lost it, it could be the undoing of us all.

"Ellie?" I heard a voice just beyond the door and jumped, nearly slipping on the slick floor. I blinked rapidly as soap dripped into my eyes, running my face under the water.

"Y-yeah?" I responded once my eyes were free of fire.

"Are you almost done?" he asked. I was sure it was Cole, though the sound of the water and the muffling through the door made it hard to tell.

"A-almost. Everything okay?" I couldn't help being slightly annoyed that he'd interrupted my quiet time and slightly worried about why he'd done it.

"Yeah, I just need to pee," he said, his voice lowering.

"Oh, okay. Um, just a second." I pumped out conditioner quickly, slopping it onto my hair and rinsing it out before it had time to soak in. I hadn't had time to shave or wash like I needed to, but I shut the water off anyway, grabbing a towel from the rack and wrapping it tightly around my body. Chaos. I forced a slow breath out of my mouth, breathing deeply through my nose. I'd learned so much from Doctor Porter. "Hurrying," I told him, though he'd not said anything else.

I ran a quick hand over my hair, glancing at myself in the fogged-up mirror. It was no use trying to look presentable in front of these people who had seen me at my worst. I opened the bathroom door, ready to step out of the room, but he held his hand up. I furrowed my brow as he placed a finger over his lips, gesturing for me to keep quiet as he nudged me back into the bathroom and shut the door.

"What are you doing?" I asked, my voice low. He lifted his phone up as I noticed it for the first time.

"I wanted to talk to you before anyone else."

"About what? Did you hear from the detective?" I stared at the blank screen, waiting to see whatever he planned to show me.

He shook his head. "No. He hasn't called yet. It's still early, though. Look, I know this isn't what you want to hear, but…" He paused as he took a dramatic breath, and the look on his face told me he was about to say what I'd prayed I'd never hear again. "We need to go back to Fallen Oaks."

"What?" I asked, my voice too loud. "What are you talking about? How can you even say that?"

He maintained a calm voice, my fear not affecting his resolve. "Ellie, I know. I know it's the last thing any of us wants to do, but if anyone can convince the group to do anything, it's you. They listen to you more than they do me."

"You ever think that's because I don't come up with idiotic plans?" I raised a brow, shaking my head at him. "How can you possibly think that's a good idea, Cole? We can't go back. What if that's exactly what *they* want?"

"We aren't helpless kids anymore, *Ellie.*" He spat my name back at me.

"Spoken like a true man. Our parents weren't helpless kids either, *Cole,*" I said his name as he'd said mine, as if I were speaking to a child. "We have no idea what we're up against. You can't expect me to get on board with this plan, let alone try to help you convince the others. Why would you even want to go back?"

He shook his head. "First of all, because when I called last night, the secretary acted like she had no idea what was going on with the case, let alone who was in charge of investigating it. It's only been five years. Only five years, and they've already given up on them. Our entire neighborhood was slaughtered, and they've already moved on to a new crime. I want to go back to remind them that we're still waiting for justice against the monsters who did this to our families. Don't you want to see their killers behind bars…or worse?"

I nodded, watching his eyes as they darted between mine. "Of course I do." He was trying to read me, as Doctor Porter often did. He wanted to know what I was thinking, where my head was. Truth be told, most of the time I had no idea either.

"Good. And secondly, I want to go back because I honestly believe it's the last thing the killer would expect us to do. Maybe, being back, we'll be able to help in some way that we couldn't as kids. Maybe we'll be able to put an end to this once and for all."

"Once and for all?" I mimicked his words. "This isn't an action movie, Cole. These are real people's lives. My life. My sister's life. Yours. Gray's. Monica's. As much as I want to see justice served for what happened, getting ourselves killed won't honor our families."

"Why do you think we're any safer here?" he asked.

I opened my mouth to answer, but shut it again. Did I have an answer to that? Truth be told, I didn't feel safe anywhere. Knowing that my parents' murderers knew where I lived terrified me, but that didn't negate the fact that this was the safest place I'd known in so long. To leave the solace of my apartment would be to go out into the unknown, into places I couldn't control like I could this one. I knew how to get out of my home. I knew where things I could use as weapons were kept and where the best hiding places were. To leave that…to venture out of my only safe space, caused my chest to tighten so much I was sure it would explode. But how could I explain that to him? How could I explain that to anyone?

The door swung open suddenly, and Cole turned around to face it as I stepped out from behind him to meet Gray's eyes. He went pink as he saw the towel wrapped around my bare body. His gaze averted instantly. "Oh, whoa. Sorry."

"It's okay," I assured him, though I wrapped a self-conscious arm around myself. "What are you doing?"

"I heard you guys talking. We all did. We didn't want to be left out of your little group meeting." He gestured to just behind him down the hall where I could see the outline of Cassie and Monica.

"We weren't—"

"It wasn't a—" Cole spoke at the same time that I did, and we both stopped, waiting for the other to continue. Finally, Cole cleared his throat. "It wasn't a secret meeting. We just didn't want to wake you."

"Clearly," Gray said, gesturing toward me, "it *was* urgent. Or do you often meet with people while you're in the shower?"

I scowled. "Cole came to me. I had no plans for any kind of meeting." I shoved past him, feeling judged though I had no reason to, and hurried toward my bedroom. I shut the door in Cole's face as he tried to follow me. "I need a minute." As I walked toward my closet, I focused on my breathing, anger getting the best of me. I pulled on a pair of clean underwear, some shorts, a bra, and a T-shirt before dropping the towel in the hamper and re-opening the door.

"So, what's this all about, then?" Gray asked. "Did you guys find something out? You were supposed to wake everyone up, that was the deal."

"Relax, Gray. We didn't find anything out. Cole wants to go back to Fallen Oaks, and he wanted me to help convince you all of that," I answered with a deadpan tone, ignoring the betrayed look on Cole's face. Monica gasped as Cassie's eyes met mine. I expected the group to immediately argue in my defense, but, at first, no one spoke.

Finally, Gray looked at Cole. "Why?"

"Because I want answers," Cole told him. He looked to the end of the hall where the girls still stood. "I mean, in the past five years—or four, at least—have any of you heard from the detectives supposed to be finding our parents' killers? Have any of you done anything but worry about when those letters—or some other reminder of the past—were going to arrive? When the killers were going to come after us next?" His gaze danced back and forth across the shaking heads, and I couldn't help shaking mine as well.

I did want to know the truth about what had happened that night, but truth be told, sometimes I wondered if we were better off not knowing. Was any sort of answer going to make us feel okay again? I highly doubted it. Was finding out it was random going to help us make sense of it? Or just the opposite, finding out that there was a reason, that in some sick way someone believed our parents had deserved what they got, was that going to help us move on? No matter what the police figured out, I wasn't sure if the knot in my stomach that had taken root since that night would ever go away. At that point, it was practically a piece of me anyway. I might miss it if it were to go.

No, I'd decided years ago that once I had Cassie with me where she belonged, we'd move on with our lives and quit looking back as much as we could. What choice did we have? Enough of our future was already being shaped by our past. Relationships, jobs, homes…everything we did would be affected by that night. I couldn't hold a job during the day because I had my therapy sessions that would sometimes conflict with the schedule. My home was equipped with two deadbolts, an alarm system, and extra locks on my windows. Relationships…well, I had long since given up on that. All I cared about was surviving. When you've faced a day where you weren't sure that you were going to make it out alive, when people very important to you didn't, survival becomes as much a desire as food or drink. It consumed my every thought. I planned my day around it. My life around it. The need to survive. When I entered a room, I planned my escape route. When I talked to a stranger, I watched their hands for the weapon they might be concealing. I was plagued with a need to survive every day as if the killer might be right around the corner, and as it was turning out, I supposed he was.

"I just don't think it's a good idea," Monica said, bringing me back to reality.

"I agree," I told her. I looked to Gray, my level-headed friend, and expected him to nod. Instead, his jaw was tight as he appeared to weigh the options.

Finally, he said, "It couldn't hurt."

"Couldn't hurt?" I demanded. "Are you serious?"

"I mean, think about it, Ellie. None of us lead normal lives." He glanced toward my hand. "None of us are married. None of us have stable jobs from what we've said. We all live our lives in fear. What could it hurt to finally have this over with?"

"It could kill us! *They* could literally kill us. Are you two even listening to this plan right now? It was a group of men who attacked our homes. Not a single person. It's not five to one. It's five to…to twenty-one!" I threw out the first number that popped in my head, though realistically I knew that number was too high, my mind racing from all the insanity. "You aren't going to play tough guy and endanger us all. If you two want to go back to Fallen Oaks, be my guest. But I'm staying here, and so is Cassie."

"No," Cole said firmly. "We stick together, whether it's here or there. That's the only request I have."

"Then it's going to be here," I said firmly. I was not planning to leave my apartment. Not any time soon, and possibly not ever. It wasn't until Cassie spoke up that I'd even considered it.

I heard her soft voice, quiet at first, but its strength grew with each word. "Ellie, what if we do go home? I…I want to visit their graves."

She was young when it happened, but not so young that she didn't remember them. Since the funeral, we hadn't been back to see their graves, despite the many times she'd asked about it. I just couldn't bring myself to do it.

I pressed my lips together, exhaling. "Cass, it's too dangerous."

"It's always going to be dangerous if we don't do anything about it. What if these letters are what helps them finally find the killers?" She shook her head, her honey-brown hair swaying over her shoulders. "Whether we're here or there, as long as the killers are running free, we'll always be in danger."

The twelve-year-old had said the one thing that the adults couldn't bear to. That we were in danger. That we'd always been. The second we left those houses with our lives, we'd put a target on our backs. The fact that we'd survived even five years since then, was likely just luck. But our luck had run out.

"She's right," Cole agreed. "We're no more safe here than we are there. They found us where we live, which means they could come for us at any time. Just like they came for them."

I looked around the hallway. Their faces seemed firm in their decision, except for Monica, who looked just as weary as I felt. "It seems as though I'm outnumbered," I said finally, shrugging my shoulders. The smell of coffee hit my nose, and I remembered the pot that I'd made as I walked past Cole and Gray and then past Cassie and Monica.

"Are you mad?" Cassie asked, her voice coming from just behind me as I poured a mug of coffee and added in some milk. I took a sip, ignoring the way it scalded my mouth as I pondered the question. The emotion in my chest *was* anger, but was I mad at her? How could I be?

"I'm not mad," I told her, looking at the others as they watched our conversation. "I just don't feel safe going back to that town. I never wanted to set foot in Fallen Oaks again, and I didn't want it for you either."

"You can't protect me from everything," she said softly, reaching out to take my hand. There was no anger in her words, just a need to be understood. And I did. As much as I hated it, I did understand. I felt the same fundamental desire she did to see our parents' graves again, to see the house where all of my early memories were made. But I knew that going back there would only bring pain.

"I know that," I said finally, because there was nothing else to say. "But that doesn't change the fact that I wish I could."

She smiled sadly, looking over her shoulder to where Gray, Cole, and Monica stood. "So, when do we leave?"

"Today," Cole said. "I want to give these letters to the police and move on with our lives as soon as possible."

"Agreed," said Gray. "I can't afford to miss much more work."

Monica was silent, her eyes searching mine as if looking for me to reassure her this was a good idea. I nodded with the men, visibly letting her down. "Fine. We should put them all in bags, too. To preserve any evidence."

They agreed, stepping forward as I pulled the gallon-sized Ziploc bags from one of the overstuffed drawers, knocking a reusable straw to the ground in the process. I picked it up, placing it back in the drawer as Cole grabbed up the letters we'd left on the counter, along with the five daisies, and sealed them in the bag together.

"What do you think the daisies are about?" I asked finally, a question that had been gnawing at me but that we hadn't discussed yet.

"Gerbera, I guess," Gray said. "Like the daisy. My mom used to plant them in front of our house all the time."

"So, it's about the name of our subdivision? Why?" I asked.

At first no one answered, but finally Cole shrugged. "I'm assuming it's some sort of metaphor." He lifted the bag higher, staring at the flowers intensely as we all watched him.

"We were innocent once," Monica answered, her voice monotonous. "And now, we're just like the daisies. Plucked from our homes, wilted, and pretty soon...dead."

CHAPTER SEVEN

October 3rd

The ride back to Fallen Oaks was a quiet one. None of us knew what to say or how to approach the situation we'd found ourselves in. Truth be told, when we'd been taken away from our homes—Cassie and I placed with our grandmother, Gray with his cousins out of state, and Monica and Cole in foster care—I'd hoped to never see those people again. Except for the occasional text during the holidays, we lost touch completely, and yet there we were, crammed into my tiny car as if we enjoyed each other's company.

We pulled into the quiet town of Fallen Oaks with a palpable sense of apprehension. The air was thick with tension, no breathing could be heard. I drove past our old high school, surprised at how small it looked compared to my memories of the place, and past the gas stations and restaurants we'd once frequented. It was funny. Somehow I guess I expected the place to look different—as if it had been affected by our absence, but to my surprise it looked absolutely the same.

Cole's phone hadn't rang, despite the fact that it was now just past noon and the detective had been given plenty of time to return our call, so we decided to head straight for the station.

We pulled up in front, my stomach clenching at the sight of the large, cobblestone staircase that led up to the old building. I put the car in park in an empty spot and remained still, questioning if we were doing the right thing. During the car ride, I'd been lost in thought, mostly tuning out whatever had been discussed as I tried to reason with myself that everything would be okay. I'd picked the skin around the edge of my fingers raw with worry, and as I stared at Gray in the rearview mirror, I started to wonder if they'd be bleeding by the end of the day. He raised his eyebrows, breaking eye contact with me to look at Cole in the seat next to him. "You ready?"

Cole nodded, putting his hand on the handle. I was shocked and a bit relieved to see that no one looked as confident as they'd seemed on the drive over. At least I wasn't the only coward.

As we all climbed from the car, taking our places next to one another to ascend the staircase in what had to be one of the most bizarre cases of déjà vu I'd ever experienced, we were silent, our bodies so close our shoulders were touching. Through it all, we'd have each other. That's what our body language was screaming. I was protected, if not by the police, by the people standing next to me. Somehow, we were in this together once again.

We walked into the crowded building and were instantly greeted by a casual-looking woman in street clothes. She sat behind a desk just beyond the door, the phone propped up between her ear and shoulder. "Just a sec," she told us, holding up a finger. After a moment, she hung up without a word to explain the strange end to her phone call. "Hi, what can we do for you?" she asked, her eyes bouncing from one of us to the other.

"Hi," Cole said, taking the lead. "My name is Cole Dennison. I called last night and spoke with someone about an old case. The...Gerbera subdivision."

The woman's eyes went wide, and it was obvious that she knew the case. Then again, who, in our town at least, didn't? "Okay..." She waited for him to continue.

"Do you know who it was I spoke with?" he asked. "We have some new information. I left a voicemail for one of the detectives, but I haven't heard back."

"Okay, sure. Let me check," she said, nodding her head and typing something into the computer in front of her. She waited for a moment before nodding. "I'm not sure who you spoke to, but I can get you with someone. If you guys will just wait here one second." She held up a finger and turned, disappearing across the room laden with desks and mounds of paperwork with officers hidden just behind them.

When she returned a few moments later, she had a very buff man with a dark goatee behind her. He grinned at them stiffly, holding out a hand to shake theirs one by one. "I'm Detective McDuffy."

"I'm Cole Dennison. This is Gray McTavish, Ellie and Cassie Delanoe, and Monica Murphy." He waved a hand in our direction as he worked his way down the line of introductions. Cole stood just a few inches shorter than the detective with shoulders just as broad.

The man waved us back, opening up a small, knee-high

gate that stood between us and the rest of the officers. We passed through with apprehension on our faces. I watched Cole trying to remain confident, but I saw him wavering. We were in over our heads. A moment that should've been filled with relief, as we were finally among people who could protect us, was filled only with agony as I was sure we were all remembering the last time we'd had to step foot in this building. The last time we'd seen all of these uniforms in one place. We were supposed to be adults, weathered by the worst things life could throw at us, but inside we were all still children who hadn't grown up a day since our lives stopped in their tracks. We made it day to day by following routines, pretending to be like everyone else, but would we ever be? I couldn't see how.

As the detective led us past a few officers working busily at their desks, he stopped in front of one and gestured that we should sit. There were only two chairs, but he didn't seem to notice until right then. He lifted one side of his mouth into an apology of sorts and looked behind him, grabbing two more from the next desk. We were still one short, but I chose not to sit. "It's fine," I told him when he moved to search for another chair.

"I'll stand," Gray told him, scooting a chair back and gesturing for me to sit. I began to argue with him, but gave up before the fight had begun. We had more important things to discuss.

"Right," the detective said, pulling out his chair so that he could sit down and type something into his computer. I was shocked by how open his 'office' was. There were no walls, just a small partition separating us from a desk just beside his. "So, what can I do for you all?" He wasn't from around there. I knew it the instant he sidestepped an opportunity to say 'y'all.' As a bona fide Southerner, it sounded almost foreign to my ears.

"Well," Cole cleared his throat, interrupting my thoughts, "we're the survivors from the Fallen Oaks murders five years ago. The ones in the Gerbera subdivision."

"I know the case well," the detective said, surprising me. He typed something else into his computer. "Got the file right here."

"Right," Cole said. I leaned forward slowly, dying to get my eyes on what the case file might say. There must've been a screen protector to keep prying eyes like mine in the dark, because his screen looked completely blank to me. "Well, as you know, we're coming up on the anniversary, and, um—" He reached back, holding out his hand. For a moment, I just stared at him. Was I supposed to high-five him? When he raised a brow at me, I suddenly realized what he was doing. I snapped to attention, reaching into my purse and pulling out the Ziploc bag full of letters. "We each received a threatening letter on our doorsteps yesterday."

The detective's brow furrowed slightly as he held his hand out to take the bag. "You all live together? Near each other?"

"No, not at all. We've stayed in contact, and when we realized we all got one, we came together," Cole answered. I was incredibly thankful he'd taken the lead on this because as I watched the detective staring at the letters through the clear plastic, I felt my stomach clenching into a knot. I wanted it all to be a bad dream—the letters, being back in Fallen Oaks, all of it.

"How much did you handle these?" Detective McDuffy asked.

"Just enough to read them. We put them in the bag this

morning to preserve whatever evidence was left. There are daisies in there, too. One for each of us."

"I see that," he said, turning the bag over in his hand as it looked like he was attempting to read the letters. "It was smart to bag these up. If any evidence is left, we should be able to find it." *Should* being the operative word there, I knew. We'd been given false hope before. "Now, did each of you file reports with your local police departments?"

"No," Cole said. "We called here first to see what we should do. When we didn't get a call back, we came straight here. There was a detective who handled our families' case before...Larry Gold. Is he still here?"

The man shook his head, confirming what we'd already been told. "Gold retired, actually. I transferred here when he left and have been assigned most of his cases. Actually, I've got all of his notes on the case." He looked back to the computer. "Were there ever any leads that you were aware of?"

I scowled. "Shouldn't you know that?"

The detective looked back at me with a smirk. "You would think. Unfortunately, the notes that Gold left behind are scarce at best. It doesn't seem like there were any suspects, even. No interviews aside from you kids." He shook his head, a look of pure confusion on his face. "That was the reason I hadn't called you back. When I received your voicemail this morning, I tried to get better acquainted with your case, but it's proving difficult." He looked at us as if we were supposed to have some answer as to why the shitty investigation had happened the way it did. When neither of us offered up any excuses for Larry Gold, Detective McDuffy shook his head. "No need to worry. I'm sure I'll find it. The rest of the notes are around here somewhere. Gold's reports are old school. It wasn't that long ago, but from what I'm learning, this station is one of the last in the county to get the latest equipment. It sucks, but it doesn't mean the files aren't here." He laid the bag down on his desk. "It just means I have to look a little harder for them. So, what we're going to do is fill out an official report on these letters, and I'll get them to the lab for further testing, see what we can find out."

"Okay," Cole said. My mouth had suddenly grown dry. *More waiting.*

"So, what are we supposed to do in the meantime?" I asked, the question apparently shocking everyone, as all five heads shot to look at me. McDuffy nodded, his eyes warm as they met mine.

"I know you're probably scared. I get it, and I don't blame you. I'm going to put a rush on these, but for right now, it's best to go back to your normal routine. Be smart, keep an eye out, but for all we know, this could be a prank."

"And when we end up dead?" I demanded, feeling anger bubbling in my belly. It was the same run around we'd been getting for years. No one knew anything, and for whatever reason, no one seemed to care to learn.

He sighed, rubbing his forehead. "Look, Miss..."

"Delanoe," I answered the question he hadn't asked.

"Delanoe." He looked at the computer and then at Cassie before returning his gaze to me. "Ellie Delanoe, right?"

I tapped my temple. "Top-notch detective work."

Again, he smirked at me, though I could tell his temper was running short as the vein where his dark hair met his forehead throbbed. "*Ellie,* I promise you, I will do whatever I can to make sure that doesn't happen."

I held his gaze, my eyes burning for me to blink, but I refused. I wouldn't give him the pleasure of looking away first. I knew from four years of working at a vet's office that to do so was to show acknowledgement of dominance. I'd never give him that. If he was going to let us die, he was damn sure going to remember what my eyes looked like when they were filled with life.

CHAPTER EIGHT

October 3rd

We walked out of the police station a few hours later in silence. Not one of us felt any better about our interaction with the police now than we had before. With nothing to do but wait, my mind raced. Could I go back home? Back to my apartment and send my sister to school the next week, go to work myself? How could we return to the normal we'd grown to know after what we'd experienced? I guess I'd thought it was impossible the first time, too, but somehow we'd found a way.

Reading my mind, probably all of our minds, Monica asked, "What do we do now?"

"I have no idea," Cole said. "Somehow I really thought that would go better than it did."

"We should've never come," I mumbled under my breath. I didn't want to fight with them, truly I didn't, but the hopelessness filling me muted any filter I'd once had.

"At least they can look into the letters," Gray said, though his tone didn't hold much more hope than I felt.

I nodded, pulling the keys out of my purse as we approached my car. "Back home, then? Back to our own homes?"

Monica let out a small whimper, and I turned to look at her. Her dark, curly hair made her pale skin look almost translucent. I stared at the blue veins under her eyes. Did she sleep as little as I did? "I don't want to be alone," she admitted. "I live alone. At least you two have each other. And they're men," she said, as if that had saved anyone we'd known before.

"What? Do you want to stay with us?" I asked her. "Don't you have work?"

"Actually, that's a good idea. I think we should *all* stay together," Gray said, his eyes locked on Monica. He shifted in place, brushing a piece of his bushy, red hair out of his eyes. He still looked so much like the teen I'd once known. The class clown that ran track and pretended he didn't care one bit about school. I knew better though. As his neighbor, I'd been privy to backyard study sessions I assumed he'd sooner die than let anyone know about. *Perhaps that wasn't the right choice of words.*

"Together? Like…for how long?" I asked, my jaw slumped open. "I have bills to pay, guys. I can't just hunker down for the next few weeks while we wait to hear back from the detective."

"Not a few weeks," Cole said quickly, "but at least a few days. Let the anniversary week pass."

"Fine," I groaned. "But I'm going back to work. You can stay in my apartment." I pulled open the car door. "And you're all chipping in for groceries."

"Could we stay here?" Cassie asked. "At least for the night? We can go home tomorrow before the anniversary. You don't work until Monday anyway." She stuck her bottom lip out. "Please. I'd like to see Grandma."

"We can't stay," I argued instantly. "We agreed we'd talk to the police. Give them the letters. That was it." I looked at each member of our group, waiting to see someone who agreed with me. "Come on," I said, when I didn't see any, "you can't tell me any of you want to stay here. Monica?" I stared at her. "You're scared to go home…miles away from this place, but you're fine with staying here?" I scoffed, looking away.

"My legs are stiff, Ellie," Cole said, stretching them out as if to prove it. "We're already here. One night won't hurt."

"One night is all it took to take everything from us," I spat. "You people have lost your minds."

"You said we could visit their graves," Gray said. He was staring at the ground, kicking a rock with the toe of his shoe, but when he looked up, his eyes locked with mine. "You and Cassie stayed close to Fallen Oaks after it happened, but the rest of us left immediately. I've not been within an hour's drive of here since then. I haven't seen their graves in years."

"We lived on the outskirts of Elkton, not inside of Fallen Oaks," I said. "And it was only for a few years until I graduated and turned eighteen. You are acting like being away from here has been a chore, but it was your choice. All of your choices."

"It wasn't our choice to become orphans," Cole said, his voice cutting through the noise. We all fell silent. "Now, you're outnumbered." He reached for my keys, taking them from my hand without permission. "We're staying. Get in the car."

Cassie called our grandmother on the way to Elkton, a small town thirty minutes outside of Fallen Oaks, to let her know that we were headed her way. She didn't mention the letters. My head bounced against the cool glass of the window as I closed my eyes and felt the familiar bumps of the roads I'd once known so well. A headache was creeping up on me, partly from lack of caffeine and partly from utter annoyance. My routine was entirely thrown off, and I had never felt more out of control than I did as Cole Dennison drove the most expensive thing I owned over potholes and around dangerous curves as if he were in a race with a teenaged version of himself.

Cassie instructed him on how to navigate the outskirts of the town, down miles of gravel roads, and toward the home where my grandmother lived alone since my grandfather's death when we were very young.

The old, yellow house looked just as it had when we left. My grandmother sat on the porch swing, her thighs toned from hours of yard work every day showing at the bottom of her cargo shorts. She stood as she watched the car pull down the drive, one hand over her brow to shield her eyes from the sun.

As Cole pulled the car to a stop in front of the garage and we all piled out, they began stretching their legs dramatically while I crossed my arms over my chest and made my way toward my grandmother.

It wasn't that she'd ever done anything inherently wrong. She was an amazing grandparent and had taken us in when we needed her most, but she was a no-nonsense woman and she'd have none of my sulking. Even after we'd just lost our parents, and she'd just lost a son, she seemed to have it all together and expected the same out of us.

The world doesn't care if you're sad, Ellie, it just keeps spinning anyway, she liked to tell us, and that was how she lived her life. Raised by two military parents, I supposed that was the only thing she knew. My dad had told me stories about her from when he was a kid and, based on those, I knew her demeanor was not likely to change anytime soon.

"Ellie, Cassie," my grandmother said, her hair a mix of dark and light gray and piled atop her head in a bun. She held one arm out, pulling each of us into a quick hug before stepping back. "What on earth are you doing back in town?"

"It's a long story, Grandma," Cassie said. "We're just here for the night. This is Cole, Gray, and Monica." She gestured toward each of them as she said their names. "They need a place to stay while we're here, too."

Grandma Cheryl nodded. "As long as you don't plan on having any wild parties. Lights go out at ten around here."

"Yes, ma'am," Gray said, stepping forward to shake her hand. She smiled at him, the warmest smile I'd ever seen on her face.

"Well, I can certainly appreciate a young man with manners." She eyed Cole. "Where are yours?"

Cole flushed red, stepping forward with an arm extended. "Sorry. Um, hi, ma'am. Thank you for letting us stay here for the night."

My grandma didn't accept his hand, turning away from him quickly. "If there's one thing I hate more than a man with no manners," she called over her shoulder, "it's one with no backbone. Come on in before lunch gets cold."

"Can I help you with dishes?" I asked my grandmother as I entered the kitchen. The small house hadn't changed a bit since we'd left, though the woman standing in front of me had aged several decades in the course of just a few years.

"You can do 'em yourself, if you wanna," she said, her voice harsher than her eyes. She stepped back, handing over the green and yellow sponge and leaning against the countertop. I stuck my hand in the scalding sink full of water and grabbed a plate.

"How have you been?" I asked. I was never one for small talk. My uneasiness made even the most normal situation awkward. Despite having lived with this woman for years after my parents' death, she was no more familiar to me than Cole, Gray, or Monica. The years after the murders were still a blur of panic and grief. Losing your parents at any age is unimaginable, but losing them as a teenager, when you're just starting to get the hang of the kind of person you're going to be...well, I wasn't sure you could ever come back from that.

In a way, it was as if my life had halted on that day. The days kept going, but somehow I seemed to have stopped. I wondered if my grandmother felt the same about herself. My father was her only child, after all.

"Why are you here, Ellie?" she asked, cutting straight through to the root of what we needed to discuss.

"I...um," I ran the dish in my hands under the stream of water and placed it into the drainer, "I think someone might be after us. Again." I met her eyes for just a moment, hoping to see a flicker of some emotion—any emotion. Was that where I'd gotten my emptiness from? I couldn't be like her, even with the darkness inside of me. I knew how to love, though it caused me severe anxiety at the thought of the vulnerability it gave me. I loved my sister more than anyone, myself included. Cassie required more of me than I would give anyone else, but I'd never seen my grandmother offer any semblance of vulnerability to anyone. She wasn't mean, I suppose. Just…cold. Empty. We hadn't had much of a relationship with her before my parents' death—I assumed that was why—but it didn't stop me from wondering about her relationship with my father.

How could someone as loving as him have come from someone like her?

"What do you mean?" she asked finally, reaching up and shutting off the water. I let the sponge drop into the sink, wiping my hands off on my shirt.

"Someone left letters at our doors. All of us. We think it was the same group of people who killed Mom and Dad." I sucked in a breath. It never got easier to say.

"What kind of letters?" I couldn't tell if she was taking me seriously, but she hadn't completely shut me down yet, which I took as a good sign.

"It was like…a poem. It said that our luck had run out and they put daisies in the envelopes. Five of them. With the anniversary on Monday, I can't see what else it could possibly be about. It's not just a coincidence that all five of us received them." I was defending myself before she'd even had the chance to tell me we were being ridiculous. It didn't feel ridiculous until I'd had to explain it to her.

My grandmother crossed her arms and gave a soft, "Hmm." When she met my eyes again, her expression had softened only slightly. "Do you still have them? The letters?"

I shook my head. "We gave them to the police."

"What did they have to say?" she asked, opening the cabinet beside her head and pulling down a coffee mug.

She filled it from the pot that was always full and took a sip.

"Who? The police?"

She nodded.

"Oh, well, nothing yet. They…they said that they'd look into it. The detective who was handling the case, Detective Gold, he retired."

"No surprise there. He should've been gone years ago," she said. When I stared at her strangely, she elaborated. "I went to school with Larry. He was a few years younger, but a nutcase, even then. How he ever managed to get himself onto the police force is beyond me."

"The new detective is looking into everything. He said he'll call us when he knows more."

She shook her head, sucking on her teeth for a moment as her gaze traveled across the room. "You kids shouldn't stay here long," she said, and I wasn't sure if she meant at her house or near Fallen Oaks.

"I don't plan on it," I said, either way. "I hate being here." I didn't have to apologize for saying so. My grandmother wasn't the kind of woman to be offended by a casual statement like that. I did hate being there. In the house filled with so many painful memories. So near the town filled with even more.

She took another drink of her coffee before setting the mug down on the countertop. It seemed as though she was going to walk away, and I saw my window of opportunity closing. "I never asked you this before," I said, speaking too quickly. "I never…I guess I never knew how to bring it up." I paused. "But, I want—no, I need to know. Did Dad ever… did he say anything? About…I mean, did you have any reason to believe…like," I couldn't make the words form, "do you know why it would've happened? Was there any reason?"

She'd been standing away from the counter but she sank back into it at my words. "Any reason?" Her stare was blank as she waited for me to go on.

"I just wonder…it seems so random."

"Their deaths," she confirmed. It wasn't a question, but I nodded anyway.

She seemed to think about her answer for a moment, and more than anything, I was grateful that she didn't dismiss the suggestion right away. I'd thought about it long and hard, though it made me feel like a horrible daughter for doing so. The very idea made my heart ache. How could my sweet, loving parents have ever done anything to warrant what had happened to them? "Everyone seems to think that maybe they did something to have caused it."

Her eyes narrowed at me. "What do you believe, Ellie?"

"I don't know. Sometimes…it's like I can't remember them fully. Like, the memories start to get hazy and I can't remember the way Mom laughed or the way Dad smelled. It —" I stopped. I wouldn't allow myself to cry in front of her. The last time I'd done it, she'd slapped me across the face. Crying showcased my weakness, and weakness was something I had to keep hidden. "I just…I wonder if maybe my memory of them is tainted because of my loss. If the people I remember are really just the best versions of the people that existed."

"Your parents weren't perfect, Ellie. No one is." I waited for her to go on, but she remained still. Her gaze traveled to the floor, and I realized it was the first time I'd seen her looking anything but cold and powerful.

"What does that mean?" I asked.

"Exactly what I said. You remember them the way you remember them. You shouldn't let anyone change that. Whatever your parents did or didn't do, they were still your parents. And they loved you. Standing around asking about who they were in comparison to the people you remember isn't doing anyone any good."

I swallowed. It felt as though she was scolding me, even if that wasn't her intention. But why wouldn't she answer me? Did she know something more than she was letting on?

"I know they loved us," I admitted. "And I loved them too. Of course I did. I just...sometimes I wish I had a reason for all of it."

"Reasons wouldn't make it any better." She pursed her lips. "No one deserves to die like they did. And no one deserves to lose everything the way you five have. Especially not a bunch of kids." It was the first thing she'd ever said to me that sounded mildly sympathetic. I let her words sink in, trying to decide how to continue the conversation when it seemed like I was being met with roadblocks at every turn. Before I came up with a solution, she pushed off the counter. "Finish those dishes up, would ya?" With that, she was gone.

CHAPTER NINE

October 3rd

That evening, the five of us gathered by the pond behind my grandma's house. We'd settled in as much as possible, but I was still on edge. I hadn't told the others about my conversation with my grandmother as I was still trying to piece it together myself. Truth be told, I was fed up with all the mysteries and secrets. I just wanted to get out of that area as quickly as I could. When the evening hit, my grandma retired to her room, demanding that we not disturb her. I could picture her sitting next to her window in the old, wooden rocking chair. She'd be reading a book, squinting because she refused to wear her readers, with her favorite shawl draped around her shoulders if I had to bet. It was about the only 'grandmotherly' thing about the woman who'd raised me the last two years of my childhood.

"Well, I see where you get your ice," Cole said, giving me a wink. I rolled my eyes, not at all in the mood for his games.

"My grandmother isn't icy just because she doesn't fall for your charms," I retorted.

"Whatever you say, Delanoe," he teased. "So, down to business..." He spoke as if he'd summoned us to a corporate meeting, and for the first time, I saw how well he must fit into that setting. Suddenly, the suit that he'd been wearing when he arrived at my apartment the day before made sense. "I still haven't heard from Detective McDuffy, and I know that we're all anxious to get home, but I'm thinking maybe we could hurry that along by doing some investigating of our own." He cracked his knuckles loudly.

"What are you talking about?" Gray asked, doubt in his voice for the first time. For once, he wasn't so eager to play Cole's doting mutt.

"I mean, nothing crazy, but why can't we look into it ourselves? We were the only witnesses, after all. Why can't we put all of our memories together and do some digging."

"Because it's a suicide mission," I argued. "Especially when we're all already on the radar of the psychos who killed our families. You can't be serious about thinking that's anywhere near the realm of a good idea."

He shook his head, obviously in disagreement. "Look, I know we're all freaked out about the letters. And, I guess I was at first, a bit more than I am now. I mean, what if the detective's right? What if it's just some stupid prank?"

"Are you willing to bet our lives on it?" Monica asked, taking the words straight from my mouth. We seemed to be at odds. No one necessarily agreed with Cole, but no one—excluding me—seemed to want to come out and say it. I watched him narrow his eyes at us, practically hearing the wheels in his head turning.

He let out an exasperated sigh. "Look, even if it is the

killers who sent the letters, what exactly are we accomplishing by sitting around and waiting for the cops to solve a crime they've obviously given up on? Why are we any safer than if we do some digging ourselves? They've already found us. For all we know, they already know where we are right now. The only way to know for sure that we're safe is to see them put away for good."

It was a sound argument; I couldn't deny that. What he was saying was absolutely true, but we had no investigative skills to speak of. How were we supposed to find anything when the very people who were trained and paid to do so, hadn't been able to? What could we do differently?

"What did you have in mind?" Gray asked finally.

"I want to go back to where it happened. I want to ask around about things we haven't been able to find on the internet. Starting with what people in town heard after we left."

"What do you mean, what they heard?" I asked.

He looked at me as if I hadn't caught onto the obvious, then after a pause, went on. "People around here have to know something. Why did so many of them stay? An entire subdivision was slaughtered just a few streets down from half the town, and no one left. Don't you think that's odd?"

"What are you saying, Cole?" Monica asked. She'd stepped closer to me, and a chill ran down my spine as her voice startled me.

"Do you think they were in on it? The entire town?" My brow furrowed, my distaste for what he was saying obvious. "Don't you think my grandma would've mentioned it? And... why? Why would our parents be the targets? That doesn't make any sense." It was the question that had haunted me for so long, and I so desperately wanted to know the answer.

"Our parents were the targets regardless of who the killers were, so it already makes no sense. I've gone over it so many times. They had no real connections, aside from their neighborhood. They worked different places, and it wasn't like any of them were friends. So, what? Was it random? Does that make any of us feel better?"

"What reason could there have been?" Gray asked, one hand in the pocket of his jeans as he shifted uncomfortably.

Cole scratched his forehead, letting out a sigh. "That's what I want to find out, because there obviously was one. I just...I can't believe it was random."

"Well, whatever it was, I'd suggest you all put your noses away and get away from that town for good." The voice came from behind us, and I jumped as a small squeal escaped my throat. I spun around to face my grandma, unaware that she'd left her bedroom, let alone that she was overhearing our conversation.

"What?" I asked, surprised by her words.

She folded her leather-like arms across her wrinkled chest. "You heard me. You all shouldn't be snoopin'. You're just asking for trouble at this point. We've already had this discussion, Ellie. You need to leave well enough alone." My grandma hadn't tried to keep it a secret that she thought us returning home was a mistake, but her words seemed to hide more than what she'd previously let on. I was now more certain than ever that she wasn't saying something. What did she know?

"Because of the letters?" I asked.

She shook her head, looking back over her shoulder as if someone else may soon join our conversation. But who? "No, because that town isn't safe for you kids, and this one ain't much better, either. I expect the letters were a way to get you here, and you did just what they wanted."

"What are you talking about? *They* who?" Cole asked, his tone demanding. He took a step toward my grandma who had her eyes narrowing at him. He had at least a foot on her in height and a good one hundred pounds, but my guess was she could've taken him if it came to it. He'd do well to watch his attitude.

"*They* whoever killed your families," she said, shrugging, though her eyes remained locked on his. Finally, she looked to me. "Now, you can stay the night, but I think tomorrow is a good day for you all to head home. No use staying around here and digging up old memories. They're gone, and nothing you learn about them will change that."

"What aren't you telling us? What would we learn about them?" I asked, cocking my head to the side. I could see a glint of knowledge in her eyes—something I'd never seen before. The years that we'd lived with her, she'd never suggested she knew any more than we did, but that seemed to have changed now.

"My guess is…nothing good," she said simply, turning on her heel and trudging back up to the house without another word.

CHAPTER TEN

October 3rd

I woke up in the middle of the night to the sound of the whirring fan above me. We were all camped out on the floor of the bedroom Cassie and I had once shared, though we'd let Cassie sleep on the lone twin-sized bed for the night.

The remaining four of us were huddled together on the makeshift pallet I'd thrown together. The room was too warm, the air sticky with sweat. I pushed my heels against the carpet, trying to wiggle out from between Gray and Cole, suddenly feeling like I couldn't catch my breath.

Gray stirred, but in the end it was Cole whose eyes opened slowly, just barely visible in the moonlight from the window on the far wall. He sucked in a deep breath, stretching his arms up above both our heads. "What's up?" he whispered, looking around the room quickly as if he'd just realized where we were.

I shook my head, keeping my voice low as I answered.

"I'm just thirsty." As I slid out from under the covers and tiptoed across the thick carpet and toward the door, I heard him moving as well. I opened the door and stepped out into the cool hallway, immediately noticing the extreme temperature difference. He was close behind me, his hand on my back as he ushered me out the door and shut it quietly. "You didn't have to come with me," I told him, shocked by how close to me he was standing.

"I don't want you to be alone. *Any* of us to be alone," he said. "Let's just go."

"Thank you," I mumbled under my breath, walking to the kitchen and feeling slightly like a child. I flicked on the kitchen light, my eyes closing involuntarily from the shock of the transition. When I was able to open them again, I padded across the linoleum floor and opened the refrigerator. I grabbed the jug of filtered water, having always hated the taste of the well water available at my grandma's house, and poured it into a glass. I turned to Cole. "Do you want some?"

He nodded slowly, apparently still half asleep. "Do you think we're ever going to know the truth?" he asked suddenly. When I glanced back, he was staring at the floor.

I set the jug down and turned to face him, leaning my back against the counter. "I don't know," I told him honestly. "I'd like to think so, but…it doesn't seem like it."

"How are we supposed to go on living without knowing the truth?" His eyes met mine and, perhaps for the first time, I noticed the vulnerability he so rarely portrayed.

"Same way we already do, I guess." I lifted the jug from the counter with a sigh and placed it back into the refrigerator.

He scoffed. "I don't know if I'd call this living."

I grimaced as I heard my grandma cough from her room just down the hall and nodded toward the front door. "Let's talk out there."

He followed my lead without a word. I opened the front door carefully, trying to keep our noise to a minimum, and closed it back after he stepped through. We made our way toward the front porch swing, and he waited until I'd sat down before he followed suit.

"What do you do, Cole?" I asked. It was a question I felt like I should know the answer to, but I didn't. The truth was, none of us knew anything about each other, despite having such a huge part of our lives tied together. We were strangers, practically. A large rift had melded that part of our lives into one and then, just as quickly, we'd run from each other in separate directions. I'd be lying if I said I hadn't hoped I'd never have to see the group again.

He pinched the bridge of his nose, rubbing the inside corners of his tired eyes. "I work front desk at a hotel." I nodded. Though it wasn't what I'd expected him to say, it did explain the suit he'd been wearing when he'd come to my apartment. "What about you?"

"Just…reception for a vet's office," I said.

"You used to want to be a vet yourself," he said, looking over to stare at me. I was surprised he knew that, though I'd never been shy about that dream.

"I can't believe *you* knew that."

He laughed under his breath, and I realized it was the first time I could remember hearing him laugh. "You do know I knew you before all of this, right? You were the girl that dressed up as a vet every year for Halloween in elementary school."

I rolled my eyes. "Yeah, well, things change. I just never thought you'd be someone who'd remember anything about me."

He shrugged. "You aren't hard to remember."

I narrowed my gaze at him, shocked by his words. It was the first time he'd ever attempted to flirt with me—at least, it felt like that's what it was supposed to be. He was lying, of course. Before all of this, I was anything but unforgettable. I'd always been plain—not horrible looking, but never one to stand out or get noticed. My mousy brown hair and freckles, paired with the extra weight that had always had a place around my waist, and the fact that I hid the one decent thing about my features—my silver eyes—behind thick frames most of the time, I was hardly one to be picked out in a crowd. Suddenly, it hit me what he was trying to do, and I scooted away from him on the porch swing.

"What are you doing, Cole?"

He shook his head, his hands clasped over his knees, his feet pushing us back and forth on the swing. "What are you talking about?"

"You think that you can flirt with me a little, and I'm so desperate to get a little attention that I'll give in and take your side in the whole staying-versus-going thing? Is that what this is?"

He furrowed his brow, his gaze locked with mine. "*What?* No! Of course not."

"You're obviously lying," I said plainly. "And it's not going to work, so you can give it up. I will always believe we need to go home. First chance I get, I'm taking anyone who wants to leave, home. If you want to stay, you can Uber."

"You'd really leave me here?" he asked, his voice filled with hurt.

"You're endangering us all with this little mission of yours."

"That's not why I'm doing this, Ellie. For the record. That's not why I said what I said. I stand by it. You were, and always have been, unforgettable. And I don't want to put anyone in danger. I just…I remember the people that we were before all of this. We had dreams and goals. I feel like I'm barely living, just waiting for the other shoe to drop. I can't…" He paused, his jaw tight as he looked out over the yard. "I can't live like this much longer."

"So, what are you saying?" I asked.

"I'm saying I need more out of life than just surviving."

I patted his chest, taking a sip of water from the glass in my hand and turning back toward the door. "Sometimes surviving just has to be enough, Cole."

"You can't honestly believe that," he argued before I had a chance to reach for the door handle. "That's all you want? For you? For Cassie? No true future? You don't think you both deserve better?"

"Of course I do. I want everything I've always wanted for both of us—all of us—but it's too late for us. We aren't one of the lucky ones. We survived something horrific, and yes, most days, it feels like that's all we get to do…survive. But so what, Cole? Most of the people we know didn't get so lucky. If surviving what happened is all that Cassie and I get to do with our lives, I have to be okay with that."

"I can't just be okay with it, Ellie. I can't. I've tried."

"When you're used to a god-like experience, it's hard to be humbled down to the same level as the rest of us," I said softly. It was a thought, really. I hadn't even meant to say it out loud, but there it was. He stared at me, his mouth agape.

"I was never a god, Ellie. I was just a kid. Just a stupid kid."

"Well, we aren't kids anymore," I told him firmly. "And we can't act impulsively. I want to find the killers. Honestly, I do, but if it means putting everyone's life in jeopardy just to do it, I can't take that risk."

He nodded slowly, as if realization was striking him. "That's why they all listen to you."

"What? Why?"

"You're a natural leader," he said matter-of-factly. "I always took the role because it was instinct for me, but it should be you. You obviously think more clearly in these situations. I'm blinded by my rage about every part of our situation. What the hell did we do to deserve this? What did any of us do? How is this fair, Ellie? How can you stay calm when the world is falling apart around us?"

I supposed his sleepiness was causing his blunt words. "I'm not calm. I'm furious at our situation, and I'm not a leader, Cole. I don't want to be. I just want to protect us all and get back home."

"Do you think we're safer at home, though?" He put up a hand to show his innocence. "I'm not arguing with you, I'm honestly asking. They found us there. I'm just wondering if you believe they would hurt us here but not there."

My lips quivered as I answered. "To be honest, I'm not sure if we've ever been or will ever be safe. But I feel the *most* unsafe here."

He nodded. "Then, we'll leave."

"Just like that?"

"I heard what your grandma said. And now I hear you. Despite what I want, I have to put the group first. Like you." I took a sip of water, feeling more nervous than ever. "I thought that's what you wanted," he said, obviously reading my expression."

"It is," I admitted. "Now, I just have to hope I'm right."

CHAPTER ELEVEN

October 4th

The next morning, we got our first bit of potentially good news. A print on two of our letters had come back as a match for a partial print from the Gerbera crime scenes—a fingerprint that didn't match our own. Despite the fact that the print did give the detectives some new information to work with, I couldn't help feeling a bit overwhelmed with the realization that this meant our theory of it being just a prank was null and void. Not that any of us had truly believed it anyway, but it had been nice to have that piece of hope to cling to in the back of our minds. There was no doubt about it now, though—we were in danger.

True to his word to me on the porch, Cole announced that morning that we would be heading home. My grandma seemed relieved to see us packing up our things, though she hadn't had much to say. She made us a simple breakfast of toast and some scrambled eggs, for the road, but it didn't seem like any of us had much of an appetite.

"We can go see their graves before we leave, right?" Cassie asked as we walked out the door that morning, headed for the car. She looked at Cole, who, to my surprise, looked at me.

"I, um—" Four sets of hopeful eyes met mine, and I knew I had no real choice. "Yes, we can. Quickly, though. I want to get on the road before evening." I tossed mine and Cassie's bag into the trunk, waiting until the three others fell on top, and closed it.

It was Gray's turn to drive, and he took the keys from me as I handed them to him, headed for the driver's side with slight apprehension. It was a bittersweet moment for all of us, I believe. Wanting to see the graves, and yet dreading it all at once.

We rode in silence, listening to the whirring of the engine and the wipers as dust from the gravel roads clouded the windshield. I was tired, unable to control my yawning that seemed to cause a chain reaction around the car. Cole watched his phone anxiously, hoping to hear more news from the detective.

As we pulled into the only cemetery in Fallen Oaks, I was filled with a sense of foreboding. I hadn't seen my parents' gravesite since the day of their burial, and though it was partially because we hadn't come home, there was another big part that was afraid to see it. I had pictured the way their tombstone would look, my grandma had even sent me a picture when it was ordered, but seeing it for myself…it would make it feel final somehow. I knew that sounded silly. They were dead, there was no changing that. But I guess some part of me felt like if I didn't ever acknowledge it, maybe I'd wake up from the nightmare at some point.

We climbed from the car, trudging across the dewy grass

and splitting up silently. Cassie took hold of my arm with both of hers. She was shaking—or maybe that was me. I remembered the last time I'd walked this same path, the footsteps identical to the ones I took then. I passed by a few familiar names, running my hands over the tombstones as I went.

As I looked ahead, scanning for the area where I knew they would be, my eyes landed on the black stone. It took my breath away. Literally, I gasped for breath as I stared at my parents' names—my last name—carved into the ebony rock. Cassie followed my gaze, her memories likely a bit more foggy than mine, and upon seeing their names she released my arm and bounded across the cemetery toward our parents' final resting place.

I arrived a few moments after her, sinking onto my knees beside where she sat. We didn't care about the dew in that moment, or about the imminent threat we faced. I didn't look to see what the rest of the group was doing. As I sat in front of my parents' headstone, the only proof I had that they'd even ever existed, I began to openly weep. I traced my pale, shaking finger over their names, picturing the warm way my mother would look at my father when they came home from a date night. I heard my father singing in the morning as he made coffee. Oh, how I missed them. I wasn't sure I'd let myself admit it until that point, but suddenly, my heart ached for them in a way I'd never experienced before.

I'd replayed that morning in my head over and over, seeing the men enter my parents' room, hearing her screams. I should've done something. I should've tried to stop them. Those were the thoughts that haunted me, every possible scenario running through my head. But I hadn't. And maybe if I had, Cassie and I would be dead, too. That was the belief I clung to with every fiber of my being. It had to be true… because if not, I'd killed my own parents.

The cemetery was silent, each of us lost in our own mourning, so when I heard a noise in the distance, the crack of a tree limb in the woods just past the cemetery, my gaze shot in that direction instantly.

I stared into the woods, squinting my eyes as if to improve my vision. I didn't see anything at first, but a cold chill ran down my spine because suddenly, nothing felt right. As I saw a dark figure looming between two trees, my vision focusing finally, I swallowed. We'd walked right into their trap.

CHAPTER TWELVE

October 4th

I stood without thought, jerking Cassie's arm and darting across the cemetery as quickly as humanly possible. My ballet flats sank into the wet grass, but I didn't care. I couldn't look back to see if we were being followed. All I knew was that I couldn't stand there and wait for something to happen.

As the others saw me running, they took off toward the car in their own runs. Fight or flight—it was ingrained in us, having saved our lives before.

My heart pounded in my chest as cool sweat gathered around my brow, every part of me on fire as I ran for my life. For all of our lives. Gray pulled the keys from his pocket, hitting the button on the fob so our doors would unlock and we catapulted into the car, Cassie landing on my lap and Cole and I banging heads. Monica shut the passenger side door, and Gray turned around, placing one hand on her seat so that he could back out effortlessly. Gravel flew all around us, dust surrounding our car so I could no longer see the treeline. I waited for someone to bang on our windows as we moved, ready to kill us all right there, but nothing happened. Instead, we whipped out of the cemetery and onto the road with lightning speed.

Gray looked at me in the rearview with an expression of pure shock.

"Everyone okay? What happened?"

I nodded. "We're fine." It felt like a lie somehow. Were any of us truly okay? "But someone was watching us in the woods."

"Someone?" Monica asked, fear filling her voice as her wide, blue eyes narrowed on mine. "Someone who?"

"I don't know. I couldn't tell. They were back in the woods. I really only saw their outline." I didn't tell them everything, though I don't know why. I couldn't bring myself to say that it had looked like the figure was dressed all in black, just like the men who'd killed our parents. Somehow that just seemed like too much.

"They were waiting for us," Cole said angrily, pounding his fist against the inside of the door. "They knew we'd come." He didn't say it, but I wondered if he was blaming himself for not believing my theory. For putting us all in danger by returning.

"Well, if they know we're here now, and there is a *they,* we're all in even more danger than we realized," Gray said, his voice full of fury as he wiped the sweat from just above his eyebrow. "We need to tell the detective what happened."

"I agree," I said, my stomach in knots as I realized what he was saying was true. If they'd somehow missed our return, they knew about it now. They were coming for us.

"Holy shit," Cole whispered suddenly. I looked over at

him, expecting to see him staring at his phone as he'd just pulled it out to call the detective. Instead, I followed his gaze, realizing that we'd taken a different way to leave the cemetery.

I stared out at the old subdivision—or should I say, *former* subdivision—in awe. It was *gone.* Each one of the twenty-something houses that had once lined our street had been flattened, the rubble cleared away. The paved streets had been torn up, and even the entrance that had once boasted two large brick pillars that announced the name of the subdivision was completely gone. Our home was now a field, no sign left that they'd ever been there. In fact, if not for the familiar look of the surrounding subdivisions and the large, white house-turned-museum just across the road, I might not have even recognized the land.

"What did they..." Gray trailed off, the end of the sentence never coming, but it didn't need to. We all stared in horror as the car came to a stop near the curb. We should've kept going. We didn't have time to stop. I knew that, but somehow my rational mind had stepped out, and all I could think about was the fact that everything I once knew was gone. Wiped from the earth in just five years.

We stared into the distance, my eyes darting across the fresh green grass covering the pavement that had once been coated with blood. There were new trees that had been planted everywhere, freshly landscaped greenery. It was like we'd never existed.

"What did they do?" Gray whispered. No one responded as we all took it in.

"I guess it would be kind of hard to sell the houses... after..." Cole trailed off, not needing to continue.

We climbed from the car without saying anything

further, walking along the grass-lined concrete with apprehension. I stepped onto the mossy lawn, holding Cassie's hand without realizing I'd taken it as we walked toward the spot where our house once stood. There was a small lump in the grass, a bit of a hill where the ground rose a bit higher than the space next to it. It could've easily been overlooked if you weren't searching for it. That was the only proof left that the house we'd grown up in had stood there once.

"I can't believe it's gone," Cassie whispered, her hand squeezing mine a bit more.

I nodded, feeling a cool tear drift down my cheek that caught me by surprise. "I can't believe *they're* gone," I admitted, my voice cracking as I spoke. I bent down, releasing her hand as I touched the mossy landscape. I ran my hand across the lump where our front porch should've been. It felt surreal. I'm not sure what I expected honestly…not anyone else to be living there, but still…the fact that they'd erased them felt cruel.

"You shouldn't be here." A voice came from just to my left, and I looked over. I hadn't seen the girl approaching. She was small and blonde, a few years younger than Cassie if I'd had to guess. Her dark brown eyes bore into me, and I realized she looked familiar, but I couldn't seem to place her.

"I'm sorry," I said after a moment of silence. "What did you say?"

"I said you shouldn't be here," she said again, her expression stone. She had dirt caked under her fingernails, her hair appeared unbrushed, and her eyes lacked a healthy shine. *She looked dead.* The thought hit me without preparation, but it was true. "You need to go." She looked behind her as if she expected someone to appear. Suddenly, she turned, running back into the woods that had once been our solace.

"Wait!" I called after her, watching as the green jacket she wore disappeared into the woods. I lunged forward, ready to rush after her, but Cassie held my arm. I turned around, waiting for an explanation. "She's getting away!" I screamed.

"Don't go after her," Cassie begged, her voice filled with panic. "Please don't leave me."

Tears filled her brown eyes instantly, and her fear caused me to stop in my tracks. I'd been ready to chase the girl down, but my sister had realized the danger I could've put us in.

"I'm not going anywhere," I assured her, stepping toward her and pulling her face into my chest. I stroked her hair, whispering in her ear as I watched the other members of our group jogging toward us. I wasn't sure what they'd seen. To be completely honest, I wasn't sure what I'd seen.

"What's going on?" Monica asked, staring between us with worry.

"Why were you yelling?" Cole added.

"You didn't see her?" I asked them, looking at each of their faces as I confirmed what I already suspected. They'd been lost in their own grief, just as I had when she appeared. "There was a girl. From the woods."

"A girl?" Cole asked, looking over my shoulder into the woods. "What do you mean?"

"She was...young. Younger than us. And dirty. She said we shouldn't be here."

"Where is she now?" Gray asked.

"She went back into the woods," I said. "I tried to stop her, but she ran off. I didn't know whether it was safe to follow her."

"Why did she say we shouldn't be here?" Monica asked, her voice an octave higher than before.

"I don't know," I said, meeting her eyes. "But I think we need to listen."

"I agree," Cole said firmly. "Let's go." He looked at Cassie. "Are you okay?"

She nodded, pulling out of my arms and wiping her eyes as we made our way toward the car. We piled in quickly, looking around us to make sure we weren't being watched. Though I didn't see anyone, in my gut I knew we were. As I climbed into the driver's seat, I could've sworn I saw a flash of blonde hair just beyond the treeline.

CHAPTER THIRTEEN

October 4th

Our next stop was one I dreaded making, though it seemed we had no choice. We pulled up to the small, red ranch without warning, and part of me hoped, as we knocked on the screen door, no one would answer.

Sure enough, after a moment's wait, the door opened and the familiar face of Kate Oliver appeared. I watched her expression change from confusion to recognition to fear within seconds as she scanned our faces before landing on Cole's. In high school, Kate and Cole had been inseparable.

She placed her manicured hands over her lips cautiously. "Oh my God."

"Hi," Cole said, taking the lead as he'd promised on this interaction.

"C-Cole?" She leapt forward, wrapping her arms around his neck quickly. "Oh my God, I can't believe it." She looked around at each of us again. "I never thought I'd see any of you again."

I had to hold in the snort I so badly wanted to let loose. More like she'd hoped she wouldn't have to see most of us again. Though Cole held only fond memories of Kate, I vividly remembered the way she and the rest of her cheerleading posse had teased me after I'd gotten my first period in class and bled through my jeans.

"What are you doing here?" she asked, the question directed at Cole.

"We need your help," he said.

She nodded. "Okay, s-sure. Come on in." She stepped back, allowing us to pass through the doorway. Her hand grazed our shoulders as if she was taking a head count as we each stepped through the threshold. "I didn't realize you were back in Fallen Oaks."

I looked around her home, unsurprised at how perfect it was. A quaint fireplace sat in the middle of the light and airy living room. I hadn't bothered to keep up with anyone from Fallen Oaks. It was a part of my past I'd rather forget. It seemed everyone felt that way, except Cole. So when he mentioned that he'd stayed in touch with Kate and happened to know where she lived, and no one had any other options, we had little choice but to agree to visit her first.

"We're leaving today," Cole said. "We came back for a few days for the…anniversary."

She nodded. "Can I get you guys something to drink? I have green tea or La Croix."

"We're fine," Cole answered for us, though it was what I would've said too. I just wanted to get this over with. "It's really good to see you," he said, lowering his voice just a bit. It felt like we were intruding on a private conversation, but that wasn't why we were here, and I'd be there to remind Cole of that if he forgot.

"You too," she said, though I wondered if he noticed she was keeping a safe distance from him. Something wasn't right. Suddenly, the hair on my arms rose as I heard foot-steps headed down the hall. Someone else was there. Before I had time to panic, a man appeared. It took a moment for me to recognize him, because I'd never have placed him in Kate's home, but when I did, I gasped along with Cole.

"Horsey?" Cole asked, his voice filled with shock as we all stared at the boy who'd been dubbed 'Horsey' in fifth grade because of the too-large teeth that had begun filling his child-sized mouth.

He laughed, his voice deeper than I remembered. "It's just Tyler now. What, um, what are you guys doing here?" He walked across the living room quickly and placed an arm around Kate.

Cole's head jerked back. I could see the way his shoulders hunched slightly, and I knew he was hoping for more from this visit than just answers to our questions. "Are you two together now?"

Kate's gaze faltered slightly as she nodded. It was Ho—Tyler who answered. "Yes. Married for two years now." His smile was proud but condescending. He was making it known that things had changed.

"Oh, wow. Kate didn't mention…" He trailed off. "Congratulations."

"Thank you," Kate answered softly, her eyes filled with concern as she tried to lock in on Cole's gaze. "Um, so, what can we do for you guys?"

When Cole didn't answer right away, likely still processing all he was learning, I spoke up. "We drove past our old homes. We were wondering, well…what happened to them?"

"Oh," Kate squeaked, looking at Tyler and then back at me. "Um, well, after everything that happened, the county had the subdivision flattened, and they made a park there. It was…well, it was hard to drive past, you know? The houses weren't selling, for obvious reasons, and it was just painful for everyone. We'd lost you all, and it was just a memory we'd rather forget."

"Well, I'm glad you could move on so quickly," Cole said, venom in his voice. He was staring out the window dramatically, refusing to look her way. I could see the hurt on his face, and my heart ached for him.

"It wasn't like that, Cole." She looked at him and then at each of us. "It wasn't an easy decision. What happened to you all…it didn't just happen to you, ya know? It happened to all of us. We *all* mourned your losses. I know it's not the same, but this is still our town. We grew up with you guys, with all of the kids who didn't make it. Our parents knew the ones who died—your parents. What happened affected everyone in Fallen Oaks, and what we did, we did because we needed to be able to heal, too."

I understood what she was saying, the painful truth of her words evident in her eyes, but that didn't make it feel any less like they'd washed their hands of us and our stain on the town. "There was a little girl there. She said we shouldn't be there." I paused as she turned to look at me. "Any idea what she meant?"

She shook her head. "I don't know. It's an open park…"

"Maybe they closed it because of the anniversary tomorrow?" Tyler offered, looking at me with less fury than he'd had for Cole.

"There were no signs," Gray said.

"Yeah." Tyler looked at Kate before he continued. "People

don't really *go* there. Not that I've seen anyway. Aside from Mr. Winters."

"Mr. Winters?" I asked, furrowing my brow. Why would our old history teacher be visiting the park where our families had died?

"Yeah, he retired a few years ago. He volunteered, or I don't know, he was elected..." Kate shrugged. "He's the new groundskeeper for the park. Tyler's right. He's the only person I've ever seen there."

"Do you know where we could find him?" I asked. I couldn't explain it...nothing about the anxiousness I felt made any sense, but I knew it in my bones. I needed to find the little girl. I needed to find out what she knew. Mr. Winters may have been our only chance.

Kate twisted her lips in thought. "Um, well, he still lives over on McKinley Avenue. The white house with the red shutters and the really big oak tree in the front. You remember?"

I nodded, though I wasn't sure if the question was aimed at me. "Thank you," I told her. She nodded but chewed her lip suddenly as she began to think aloud.

"You know, I probably shouldn't say anything, but...well, if I don't..." She sighed. "I don't know. It's silly, I guess."

"What is it?" I demanded, irritated at her for wasting a second of our already pressed time.

"It's just...maybe she was talking about the curse. I mean, being here could put you all in danger." She looked at us as though we should know what she was talking about, but as I looked at each of the members of my group, I knew we were all on the same page: lost.

"Curse? What curse?" I asked.

She furrowed her brow, her eyes landing on each of us

before she looked at Tyler. "They don't know," she told him. He seemed less shocked than she obviously was.

"I'm not surprised, honestly. I never really heard much about it until everything had already happened. I think the adults tried to keep it quiet as much as they could," he told her.

"What are you talking about?" I demanded, calling their attention back to me. "Someone needs to tell us. We don't have much time." I thought then about my boss and the massive apology I was going to owe him if I didn't show up to work on Monday. We all had lives to get back to, and staying there solving puzzles wasn't exactly high on my list of priorities. But what choice did we have? It seemed like the puzzle had to be solved in order for us to return to normal—or our semblance of normal, anyway. How likely was I to forget about the girl anytime soon if I didn't have some form of an answer? And I couldn't live any more paranoid than I already was.

Tyler and Kate stared at each other, their expressions carrying a conversation we weren't privy to. Finally, Kate sighed, looking back at Cole. "When you all left, there were... well, rumors, I guess." She looked back at Tyler for confirmation. When he nodded, she went on. "About what happened with your parents. People said—" She offered a small laugh. "People said what happened was because of a curse from, like...I don't know, a hundred years ago or something."

"What kind of curse? What are you even talking about?" This time, it was Gray who asked the question. He had the same doubtful frown I knew I must be wearing.

"I know it's silly," Kate said, obviously reading his expression, too. "But it's what they said. Something about the land being sacred." She spoke with uncertainty, looking at Tyler as her voice raised to end each sentence with a question. "Yeah, the land that Gerbera was on. Apparently the people who settled there before the subdivision was built cursed it." She waved her hand as if casting a spell. "Anyway, it's probably just superstitious folklore, but apparently your old subdivision was on special, sacred ground, and when your families paid to have their houses built there, they caused all of Fallen Oaks to fall under a curse. They blame everything bad that happens now on..." She trailed off, stopping herself before she could finish her sentence, though she'd left little to the imagination.

"Why was it supposed to be sacred? And why have we never heard of that?" I asked. Surely something so serious would've at least been passed along to me in quiet rumors, but I could honestly say I was drawing a complete blank.

"I have no idea," she answered, shrugging one shoulder. "I'm sorry. I wish I did, but I never really believed it, I guess. I just thought, well...it's probably what the girl meant." She looked at Tyler again. "Don't you think?"

"Maybe," he said softly, his gaze apologetic.

"What do you mean?" Cole asked. "What does any of that have to do with her?"

"Well, she said you shouldn't be there because *technically*, the curse wasn't fulfilled. All of the blood of the residents of Gerbera wasn't shed." She twisted her mouth. "People believe because you didn't die, we aren't done with the curse."

"People?" I raised a brow.

"Not me," she said quickly. "Not really, anyway. The town tried to do the right thing and clean up the land. *If*, and it's a big if, anyone believed it was cursed because it was inhabited, we all hoped the fact that it's a park now would end the curse."

"So that's why they did it?" Cole asked. "Not just because it was hard for you to drive past?"

She looked at the floor. "I'm sorry. I didn't want to tell you and get you all upset. Curses…it's silly." When she looked back up, her expression told me everything I needed to know: she believed the curse was anything but silly. "But yes. When the council voted to clean up the land and forbid anyone else from living there, we were really just trying to protect you all."

I didn't believe in curses, to be honest. I was logical to a fault, but that didn't mean it didn't hold merit in my fear-filled mind. I bit my lip, wondering if our parents knew anything about the supposed curse before they died. Why hadn't anyone tried to protect *them?*

CHAPTER FOURTEEN

October 4th

Mr. Winters opened the door almost as if he were expecting us. His wrinkled lips pressed together in disappointment and he grumbled a soft, "Hello."

"Mr. Winters," Gray said, stepping forward so that he was a few feet in front of the rest of us. "I don't know if you remember us, but—"

"I know who you are," Mr. Winters cut him off. "And you'd better come inside." He held open the door, stepping back so that we could come in. I hesitated, looking back over my shoulder toward the highway as I wondered if we were making a mistake. As the four other members of my group entered the house, Cassie looked back to make sure I was coming, and I had no choice but to follow suit. That seemed like it was becoming a pattern with the five of us.

Once we were all inside of the Victorian home, Mr. Winters shut the door, turning around with a huff. "Well, you all are crazy to have come back here," he said simply.

"You're talking about the curse?" I confirmed.

His eyes widened just a bit and he nodded. "So you do know about it, then? Which means it really is just sheer stupidity that brought you back."

"We didn't know anything about any curse when we came back," Cole said defensively. "And the police never mentioned anything."

Mr. Winters rolled his eyes slightly, and he folded his arms across his portly stomach. "The police. Well, fat lot of good they are, aren't they? Well then, what can I do for you kids?"

"We want to know what you know about the curse," Cole said.

"And I wanted to ask you about a little girl I saw in the woods behind our old subdivision. We heard that you take care of the grounds out there, so I thought maybe you'd be able to tell me who she is and where she lives," I said.

"And why she'd tell us we shouldn't be there," Cassie added.

He nodded slowly, letting a long breath escape his nose. "Well, that's a lot of questions. Why don't we sit down?" He gestured toward the formal sitting room just behind us. There was only one small couch and two armchairs in the room, but we huddled together on the couch with Cole and Gray leaning awkwardly on the arms. Mr. Winters took a seat in one of the chairs and crossed one leg over the other.

"Well, then…what would you like me to tell you about first?" he asked, folding his hands together on his knee.

I stared at him blankly, shocked by his frankness. "You—you're going to help us?"

He blinked. "Well, that's why you're here, isn't it?" There

was a joyous tone to his voice that had me confused. What did he know? Why was he so willing to share it with us?

"We want to know about the curse. We want to know what people are saying about our parents and why there are no answers about what happened to them," Cole answered, his voice filled with determination that caused my belly to burn. It sounds ridiculous, I know, but for the first time, I was filled with something other than outright fear. Suddenly, I felt like I was a part of something bigger than myself…bigger than all of us. The need for answers overpowered any nerves that I had once felt.

"I see," he said, one gray eyebrow raised slightly. "And what is it you *think* you know? About the curse? And…er, your parents?"

"We don't know anything," I answered before Cole could. "But we will. If you won't help us, we'll find someone who will. We deserve to know the truth. You have to believe that."

He mumbled something under his breath that I didn't quite catch before folding his hands over his round stomach. "Well, you just so happen to be right about that, young lady, but I'll tell you this…I might be one of the only people in town who feels that way. I'd be careful who you talk to about this."

"What do you mean?" Monica squeaked from behind me. I was always surprised when she spoke up, as she was usually the quietest of the group.

"The *curse,*" he said the word with a dramatic eye roll, "isn't really talked about. And certainly not with the younger generations. Most of it at this point is just considered gossip, but to the founders of this town…it's as real as you are."

"But why do they think our families were cursed?" Gray asked.

"It wasn't your families that were cursed," Mr. Winters

corrected quickly. "No, no. It was the *land* that your families inhabited. The Gerbera Subdivision." He leaned forward in his chair, adjusting the knees of his pants as he spoke, his deep voice carrying us through the chords of his story. "See, years and years ago, back when Fallen Oaks was founded, there were already dozens of people living here. The stories vary here—some say there were tribes of Native American warriors, others say it was a prominent family, some say poor villagers, others claim it was a clan of witches. What all the stories agree on, though, is that I'm afraid the land we live on today wasn't acquired by cordial means." He clicked his tongue. "Lots of bloodshed. There was a town not too far from here where they said water ran red for days after a few of our more *outcasted* founders ventured off to find a home for themselves. They murdered thousands. Savages, they were. Rumor has it that the men who founded our town buried all of the bodies on the land that Gerbera sat on. Just before the final warrior died, he, *or she* depending on whose version of the story you believe, put a curse on the land and all who inhabited it. The founders were warned to leave the land sacred, as the final resting place of so many. And for many years, they did. When developers came in back in the seventies and started looking at building a subdivision there, the city council shut them down. Every step of the way, there was resistance. But when your grandfather was elected mayor," he said, pointing to Cole, "things changed. I don't honestly know how it happened, but it did. The subdivision was approved, and construction began. Your grandfather wasn't a bad man, I don't think, but he was blinded by greed. He knew what the subdivision on an otherwise uninhabited piece of land could do for the local economy, and he made it happen, curse be damned." He sighed, rubbing his forefinger and thumb across the crease in his freckled forehead. "Your families each bought a lot and paid to have their houses built there, though they were warned not to, and so, the...quote, unquote *curse,* began."

"Why would they buy the land if they knew about the curse?" I asked, shaking my head. It wasn't that I believed in the curse. It was ridiculous. But even still, I wouldn't have chanced it.

"They couldn't have known," Cole said defensively, "and neither could my grandfather."

"They did," Mr. Winters said gravely. "They all did. We made sure they knew."

"Who's *we*?" Gray asked.

"We call ourselves the Council of Elders. The unofficial protectors of Fallen Oaks and the ones in charge of passing on the memories and stories of our founders so that we may learn from their mistakes. The story of the man who cursed that land was passed down to me from my great-grandmother, and some variation of it has been passed down to dozens of others here. We tried to warn your grandfather and then, when he wouldn't listen, we tried to warn your parents. Your families. They thought we were ridiculous. They all did. But it happened. The curse came to fruition, just like we warned them it would."

"What? Because you all killed them?" Cole asked, standing up so quickly the couch moved with him across the hardwood floor.

Mr. Winters didn't seem shocked by his accusation, but he shook his head nonetheless. His smile was kind as he answered. "No, Cole. We didn't kill your families. We are nonviolent. Our only goal is to protect the people of Fallen

Oaks, even from themselves. So, to kill your families would be quite the opposite of that, wouldn't it?"

"So who was it, then? Do you know?" Cole asked, not retaking his seat. His jaw tightened as he waited for the blow that would be an answer.

Mr. Winters frowned, not breaking eye contact with Cole. "I don't. I'm sorry. I truly wish that I did. I've told that to the police many times. I have my speculations, of course, but at the end of the day, none of it matters."

"Why not?" I demanded.

"Because no matter who wielded the weapon, the founders were the true murderers. Your families disregarded the warnings, and they paid the consequences." He paused with a wince. "I know that sounds harsh."

"It sounds like you think they deserved to die," I said, anger welling in my chest as I stared into his dark eyes. Surely no one could be so heartless.

"Oh, my dear," he said softly. "No one ever thinks they deserve to die...and yet, we all do someday. That's the way of the world."

"What kind of fortune-cookie shit is that?" Cole demanded, stepping in front of me protectively. "Are you and this Council of Elders going to help us find our parents' murderers or not?"

"I should say not," Mr. Winters said, his voice raising slightly, though it remained non-confrontational. "It's time for everyone to just move on. The land is cleared now, and the curse has ended."

"Has it, though?" I asked, remembering Kate's words.

Mr. Winters looked my way. "What do you mean, dear?"

"If we're still alive, is the curse really over?"

"There is no curse," Cole told me. "Don't tell me you believe—"

I cut him off sharply. "Because some people don't seem to believe that it is."

"Yes, I know all about that, and you're right. Some people believe because you five inhabited the land once, you're all a part of the curse. That until you die, the curse on Fallen Oaks can't be lifted."

"But, it wasn't Fallen Oaks that was cursed at all, was it? It was our families…and if we're the only remaining heirs, us being cursed wouldn't affect any of you all, right?" Cole asked.

"It depends on who you ask," Mr. Winters said vaguely. "I know that's of very little help to you, but I'm afraid that's all I've got. Many people believe many different things. I, personally, believe the curse ended when the land was cleared. I know others who think the curse will end when you die, even others who believe the curse won't end until your bloodlines are wiped out completely."

"So, that's what the little girl meant, then? We shouldn't be there because we were in danger," I thought aloud.

"What little girl?" Mr. Winters asked, clearly forgetting the mention of her when we'd first arrived.

I started to answer, but stopped, some small voice inside of my head telling me to protect the girl at all costs. She'd gone out of her way to warn us of the imminent danger surrounding our return to Fallen Oaks, after all. I froze. *If she knew we were in danger, she must've known who was after us.* Why hadn't I thought of it before?

I stood from the couch without warning, all eyes suddenly on me. "Nevermind. We should go," I said when I realized Mr. Winters was still waiting on a response.

"Go? Go where? Surely you haven't gotten your questions answered already," he said quickly, standing up as we did.

"I think we know all we need to," I said, giving Cole a look that I hoped he'd understand, and then the same look to Gray. We needed to leave. *Right then.*

Cole cleared his throat. "Yes, right. Well, thank you for your, er, help, I guess." He rubbed his hands together in front of his stomach, turning toward the doorway and waiting until we'd each filed out of the sitting room before he followed us.

Mr. Winters was quiet, watching as we opened the door. Just before I stepped outside, I heard his voice once more. This time, his words were a warning. "I don't know how much help I was to you, though I certainly hope I was able to provide some of the answers you sought. If you take any of my words to heart, though, I hope it's these: if I were you kids, I'd get as far away from Fallen Oaks as possible. And I'd never come back."

CHAPTER FIFTEEN

October 4th

Back in our old Gerbera subdivision, the very place we'd been warned not to return, we walked along the treeline, searching desperately for the one piece of the puzzle I had yet to put together. Just who was the girl who'd warned us away from this place? She was young. Younger than Cassie. And aside from Cassie and I, no one had seen her. But she'd been there and she'd known who we were. Why? How? And were we truly in danger at all?

I'd be lying if I said I hadn't considered leaving the rest of the group in the woods, taking Cassie and leaving that place for good. Of course the thought had been there. The darkness hadn't left me, though the past few days had been enough of a distraction that I could leave it behind for a while. Still, the thoughts of death consumed me. Thoughts of dying or killing...how easy either would be.

If the curse were real, what would I do? How would I want it handled? I couldn't let them kill us. I would fight to the death to protect Cassie—I knew that deep in my soul. It would've been poetic, really, for me to bleed out on the very soil my parents had. But what would she do without me? There had to be another way.

"Did you see which direction she headed?" Cole asked. I stared at the smudge of dirt just above his left eyebrow. He was sweaty and, if I'd been close enough, I would've been willing to bet he smelled of stress sweat and fast food. We all did. Two days of cramming into my tiny car and binging on the fried food my grandmother made as well as dollar menu items on the way down had us all reeking. What I wouldn't have given to step foot into my own shower. The thought alone sent a wave of euphoria through me.

The peace was short-lived, though, as I heard a cracking noise in the distance and spun around quickly. My eyes scanned the woods, watching for movement. The rest of the group followed suit, our backs forming a circle so that we had every angle in our sights. As I watched, waiting to see who would emerge, and from where, I couldn't help wondering if everyone else had experienced the same train of thought as I had. Would they be willing to let me die—to let Cassie die—to save their own skin? I wanted to think not, but I knew it was ridiculous. Of course they would. At the end of the day, it's at the very core of who we are to be selfish, especially with our own lives. Survival instinct and all. No one would willingly die for someone else unless their own selfish motivation told them to. I'd die for Cassie because I couldn't live with myself if I lost her. Even the most selfless-seeming actions had selfish roots.

Suddenly, causing my thoughts to screech to a halt, I caught a flash of blonde hair in the distance. "Hello?" I called, my heart leaping in my chest. As I watched the blonde hair peeking out from behind the tree a little more and saw the first little brown eye, I let out a gasp. *I wasn't crazy.* At least not about this, anyway. I couldn't deny that the thought had crossed my mind—that maybe the girl had been a figment of my imagination after all, but there she was, flesh and blood. She walked out from behind the tree cautiously, her head down, hair in her eyes, and I was able to get a better look at her. She was thin—too thin—her shape gaunt, all sharp angles and shadowy cheekbones. "Hi," I called to her, taking a step forward in her direction. "Do you remember—"

"I told you not to come back," the girl said, though that wasn't technically true. "I said you shouldn't be here."

"Who are you?" Cole demanded from behind me, but I held up a finger to silence him. The girl looked up at him in fear, and I cast a warning look his way. Her eyes were wide, too big for her small face, and filled with terror as she stared at Cole. His eyes met mine, and he took a step back, seeming to read my warning.

"It's okay," I told her carefully, bending down on one knee so that I was at her level. Her eyes darted from Cole to me, and she stepped back an inch. "You don't have to be afraid of us. We aren't going to hurt you," I promised, pausing for a beat before I continued. I'd learned these tactics from my therapy sessions. I couldn't let her feel cornered. I needed to be on her level. "Can you tell me your name?"

The girl chewed on her lip with rotten teeth. It was becoming increasingly obvious that she must live in the woods. But was that possible? A girl so young, I wasn't sure she could've survived so long on her own. Finally, she shook her head. So, no name yet. "Okay, that's alright," I went on without a hitch. "Do you know who we are?" I gestured toward the rest of them as they stood behind me.

She lifted her gaze to the others before her terrified eyes landed back on me. She gave a swift nod.

"Okay," I said, feeling accomplished. "Can you tell me what you meant earlier when you said we shouldn't be here?"

Her eyes trailed down toward the ground, and she twisted her bare foot on the dirt. I stared at her filthy toenails, wondering how I'd missed them before. Then again, I'd hardly had a few seconds to take in everything about the girl last time. This time, I studied her with determination. If she ran away again, I needed to have her image burned into my mind.

"It's not good," she whispered, her voice shaking.

I paused, hoping she'd elaborate, but when she didn't, I leaned in closer. "What's not good, sweetie?"

"You." She looked over the group again, though her eyes never met mine.

"What do you mean?"

"Not good," she repeated. "I know who you are."

Seeing we were getting nowhere, I sighed, swatting away a mosquito as it landed on my arm. "Are you out here by yourself?" I asked, curiosity getting the best of me. If I could meet whoever was taking care of her, perhaps then we could get some real answers. Her eyes grew even wider, her lashes swallowing her brows completely, and she took a step backward.

"No, it's okay." I tried to calm her fears as I watched them welling inside of her. She took a sharp breath as a stick cracked underneath her feet. I waited, frozen in place as I watched to see what she would do. Without warning, she spun around, running away from me at lightning speed.

I stood up, unwilling to lose her again. My tennis shoes dug into the forest ground, giving me traction that she didn't have. Though I had much longer legs and everything working in my favor, she still managed to keep a small lead on me. She knew her way through the woods, darting, zigzagging, and ducking at the most opportune moments while I had to slow to plan out each move. Still, I kept her in my sights, moving just a few feet behind her for most of the journey.

When she went around a large tree, her small frame disappearing for a moment and not returning as I had expected, I stopped. "Hello?" I called. I took four steps forward, panting heavily as I peered around the back of the tree.

The girl was there, huddled in the bottom of the tree, where a natural opening had occurred—a nature-made hideaway. "You don't have to be afraid," I told her. "I promise, we won't hurt you."

"Ellie…" I heard Cole say my name in the distance, his tone full of concern.

"It's okay," I told him, keeping my eyes on the girl. "Would you like to come out?" I extended my hand, palm open for hers.

"No." The voice that answered wasn't one I recognized. It took a moment for it to register. "I don't think she would." I turned around slowly, my heart leaping into my chest as I stared down the barrel of a gun pointed directly at my face, and the terrifying woman that wielded it.

CHAPTER SIXTEEN

October 4th

"Who are you?" she demanded. Her strong Southern accent spoke of many years spent in the area. Just in my five years away from the Deep South, I could pick up on the lilts of her tongue and drawn out 'I's that I had long since abandoned despite being just a few hours north. She wore a worn, tan dress, and her blonde hair was unbrushed and matted with dirt.

I shook my head, my hands going into the air. "We mean you no harm," I assured her, keeping my voice as steady as possible. I felt sweat beading on my forehead, my temples pulsing.

She raised the gun a bit more, a muscle in her jaw twitching that said I would get no more warnings. "I said, who are you?"

"M-My name is Ellie Delanoe," I said softly, trying to find my resolve. Why had we ever come back to this place that had only ever brought us heartache? The gun dropped slightly at my name, and her eyes fell just behind me where I knew she must've been able to see the little girl.

"Millie, get out here." For just a split second, I thought she was mispronouncing my name, and my brow lowered as I tried to understand. Then, I heard the rustle of leaves behind me and realized the girl was coming out of hiding.

"I was only trying to help her. She...I thought she was alone."

The girl's weary eyes shifted toward Cole and Gray, standing just to my left. "Who are they?" she asked, the question still directed toward me.

"This is Cole Dennison and Gray McTavish." I gestured toward Cassie. "This is my sister Cassie Delanoe and," I gestured toward Monica last, "Monica Murphy. We...used to live here." I pointed back behind us where you could still see the clearing for our subdivision-turned-park.

At those words, the gun fell to her side completely. "You're the survivors." It was less of a question than a statement, as a look of sudden understanding filled her face, but I nodded in confirmation anyway.

"Yes, we are."

"But...what are you doing here?" she asked. "Why would you come back?"

I wasn't sure what to tell her. How honest could I be with this stranger?

Before I could answer, I heard Cole's voice. "Who are you anyway? I've never seen you before. Are you from Fallen Oaks?" His tone was harsher than I would've liked, especially given the gun she still held tightly. When she answered, her eyes never met Cole's.

"Yes, I'm from Fallen Oaks, but it's been years since you've seen me."

"None of us have been in Fallen Oaks for five years," Cole said. "Do you live here now?"

She nodded. "That way," she said, not elaborating further.

"Are you not going to tell us your name?" Cole asked, his voice filled with irritation.

She continued to stare at me, refusing to acknowledge him though she was answering his questions. The little girl clung to the woman's leg, and I became instantly sure that she must be her daughter. Their blonde hair and dark brown eyes were nearly identical. "She's beautiful," I said softly, trying to ease the tension. It was true—they both were. Despite being filthy, the girls were striking.

The woman's hard expression softened, and she rested a hand on the back of the girl's head, pressing her face into her upper thigh lovingly. "Thank you."

"We're sorry if we disturbed you both, or scared you at all. We...we came home to visit for the anniversary and ran into your little girl. I was worried she'd gotten lost and was out here alone, so I followed her. I was just trying to make sure she was safe," I told her.

The woman stared at me, her eyes taking in my appearance and obviously trying to decide whether I was trustworthy. Eventually, she sighed. "That's kind of you. She likes to wander in the woods behind our house, and she slipped away from me." She fired a sharp glance at her daughter, and I wondered if it was the first time that had happened. Based on the look she was receiving, I'd guess not.

I looked at the little girl, then, bending a few feet so I was at her level. "I'm sorry if we scared you." The girl tucked her face even further behind her mother's leg and offered no response. "Anyway, we're going to go back to the park for a while," I said, trying to test out a theory I was slowly working out in my head. "We're sorry to have bothered you." I turned slowly, much slower than I would have if I were actually planning to leave right then, but much to my relief, the plan seemed to work.

"The park?" the woman asked quickly.

I turned back around. "Yes. To say goodbye to our parents. That's where we were when we ran into Millie."

"You shouldn't be there," she warned, mimicking the warning her daughter had given us just a few short hours before. Out of my periphery, I saw Cole shift in his place, and I knew he was waiting for the same thing. They knew something.

"Excuse me?" I asked, playing innocent. "What do you mean?"

The woman moved backward half a step, biting down on her bottom lip. She glanced at the girl. "Who all knows you're home?"

Her question sent chills down my spine and, for the first time since she'd lowered the gun, I began to wonder if we were in danger. "A few people. The police, mostly."

Her eyes grew wide. "You shouldn't trust the police."

Whatever I'd expected her to say, it wasn't that. I stepped closer as if I hadn't heard her, but we all knew I'd heard loud and clear. I looked to Cole, his eyes filled with as much confusion as mine must've been. "What do you mean?"

She shook her head. "I can't say. Just...please go and get home. Far away from here."

"You can't just leave us with that," Cole said angrily, stepping in front of me so that she had no choice but to look at him. "Who are you, and what do you know?"

"I can't tell you that," she said, her voice powerless as her eyes fell to the ground. She was the only one of us with a weapon and yet, in that moment, she seemed the weakest—as if the right gust of wind might've knocked her straight off her feet.

"Why not?" Cole demanded. The group was getting restless. To my sides, I could see Gray and Monica shifting in place. Cassie crossed her arms over her chest, stepping up so that our hips were touching.

"I don't want to hurt you," she said, shaking her head. "But I can't tell you any more. I shouldn't even be talking to you."

"Are we in danger?" I asked, stepping around Cole so that I could meet her eyes once more. I couldn't let her walk away yet. I needed to know. "Could you please just tell us that?" She looked at me, narrowing her eyes as she contemplated what to say. I could see it in her expression—how badly she wanted to tell me more—but something was stopping her. "How old is your daughter?" I asked finally. "She can't be more than five or six." The woman put a protective hand around her child but didn't answer. I watched her grip shift on the gun. "My sister's twelve. She was seven when everything happened…so, not much older than your little one." I swallowed, pausing to watch her expression soften. When it did, I went on. "It was the hardest thing I've ever had to do, running out of that house while my family was dying. But I had to protect her. And that's still what I'm doing. I spend every day protecting her, just like you and your daughter. I'm not her mom, but I'm all she has left. So, you don't have to tell me your name, but please…please, if you know something that we should…I'm begging you to tell us. One mom to another." I pressed my lips together, the sudden tears that lined my eyes surprising me. Everything I'd said was true. I wasn't thinking about anyone like I was thinking about Cassie. Everything came down to protecting her.

The woman glanced down at her daughter and back up to me, her brown eyes still guarded, yet warmer than I'd seen them. "There's a lot you should know," she said finally. "But… I'm not sure I'm the person to tell you."

"You may be our only hope," I said.

"That's a scary thought," she said sadly. "Because I lost hope a long time ago."

"What do you mean?" I asked.

She sighed. "I remember you. All of you. But I haven't seen most of you since elementary school."

I tilted my head to the side, examining the features that I knew were so familiar. Who was she? Where did I know her from?

"My name's Margaret Gold," she said, and the name struck an immediate chord of recognition with me. It wasn't possible. I shook my head, stepping back as I sucked in a breath. "But he called me Daisy."

CHAPTER SEVENTEEN

October 4th

"Wait, no. You're not *that* Margaret Gold. There's no way," Cole said. I was thankful he'd spoken because no words could be formed in my brain at that moment. I stared blankly at her, memories flooding my mind of the blonde-haired, brown-eyed child that had once played tag and Red Rover with us in Kindergarten. I vaguely remembered the story of her disappearance. We were in third or fourth grade at most when she'd been taken. Everyone thought her father had something to do with it, from what I could remember, but he was never arrested. I was young, so most of the story was a jumbled mess in my mind—bits and pieces here and there that I'd picked up from the news and my parents talking about it.

She'd been walking home from school, I remember that much, and she'd never made it there. She was the reason my mom had quit her job—the reason I'd never been allowed to walk home or ride the bus home to an empty house again.

Her disappearance had set a spark of fear loose in our once-quiet town. But nobody believed she was still alive. There had been a memorial for her. We'd had our junior high yearbook dedicated to her memory.

"I can't believe it's you…" I said, the only words I could manage to muster.

"How are you still alive?" Gray asked the question I knew we must've all been wondering.

Margaret looked at him with a lifted brow. "It's a long story, and one I'd rather not talk about now, but you should go. If the police know you're here, I'm honestly surprised you're here talking to me." Her eyes grew wide. "But you can't tell them you saw me. My father can't know where to find me."

Her father. The detective who'd investigated our parents' case. Why wouldn't she want him to find her? Where had she been all this time? "We'll keep your secret," I promised her, vowing to make the others do the same, though I had no idea how I would manage that. "But you need to tell us the truth about our parents. Why can't the police know you're here?" Suddenly, a realization hit me. "Oh my God, is your…" I looked around the woods. "Is the person who took you still out here? Are you still being held prisoner?" Every hair on my arm stood up as I looked around. If that was the case, I'd put us all in more danger than I'd realized by coming there. But then again, she did have a gun. How much danger could she possibly be in? Unless she had Stockholm Syndrome. I'd heard a bit about that.

"No," she said quickly, holding a hand up. "No, he's gone. It's just Millie and me now."

"Well then, why? The police don't know you're alive?

Don't you want to find your family? See them all again?" I asked.

"No," she said stiffly. "I don't want to see him."

"Your father was a cop, right?" Cole asked, and I nodded along with her.

"You don't want to see him?" I asked. "Did he…have something to do with it? Your disappearance."

"No," she said. "Not my father. I didn't know the man who took me. Not at first, anyway."

"Margaret, you need to talk to us. Tell us what you want about your own story, it's yours, but you have to tell us the truth about ours. Whatever you know. Lives are at stake here." I sucked in a deep breath, hoping I could trust her. "Whoever killed our parents is out to finish what they started. They want to kill us, too."

She furrowed her brow. "That doesn't make any sense."

"It's all about this stupid curse. They believe if they don't kill the entire bloodline of people who lived on this land, then the town will be cursed," I said.

"*What?* Who told you that?"

"Mr. Winters. He was a teacher at our school, but…you wouldn't have met him, I guess. He takes care of the park now."

"Well, I don't know anything about that, but I'm not surprised to hear you're in danger."

"Meaning what?" I asked.

She glanced over her shoulder, then back at me. "How much time do you have?"

"How long do we need?"

She smirked slightly. "Follow me, okay?" She turned, taking hold of the girl's hand and marching ahead, lifting her legs awkwardly high so her dress didn't catch on the brush of the forest floor.

We hesitated in unison, each looking at each other before deciding to make a move. I didn't necessarily want to follow her; it seemed dangerous. But at that point, she may have been the only person who could give us any answers. Did we really have a choice? The others seemed to agree with me, their fearful eyes locked on mine as they waited for me—their suddenly appointed leader—to lead the way. I took a step forward, following the path that Margaret led us down with the others close behind.

We walked for a few minutes, twisting and turning down the dirt path, twigs and limbs reaching out and grabbing hold of our clothes as we moved. I tried to grab hold of the branches, moving them behind me easily so they wouldn't smack Cassie as she stayed close to me.

When the woods finally cleared into a small field, I stared at the house in front of us. It was small and white with rotting wood siding and a blue front door that looked ready to fall from its hinges at any moment. The front porch was sinking in, in desperate need of support, and the gutters had literal plants growing out of them. As I looked past the decay, I couldn't help noticing the fact that there were flowers planted in a makeshift bed in front of the porch. They were sloppy and wilted and it was obvious the little girl had helped, but they were there nonetheless. There were a few toys scattered throughout the large yard: a faded pink tricycle and a large, red ball immediately caught my eye. They didn't have much, but the girl was loved. Cared for. Immediately, I was put at ease. I no longer felt in danger. It's crazy, I know, but the feeling of complete safety washed over me.

"You can go play, Millie," Margaret said, stopping abruptly in the yard and pointing her away from the group. When the girl started to move, her mother held her hand, pulling her back to her to deliver one last message. "Stay in the yard."

"Okay," Millie agreed with a giggle, rushing off to chase a nearby butterfly. I watched her pounce after it, missing it by several feet each time but never giving up.

Daisy approached the small front porch, grabbing hold of the rusted, black railing and easing herself down onto the steps. "Feel free to sit," she said. "I don't have much space, but…" She trailed off, not seeming to know what else to say.

"Thank you," I said to her, shuffling my feet in place but not moving to take a seat. No one else accepted her offer either.

"I know I'm being secretive, but I don't trust people easily," she said, her watchful eyes following her daughter's movements across the yard.

"I can hardly blame you for that," I said. "It's not like any of us trust easily."

"What happened to you, anyway?" Monica asked. "Can you tell us that? Do you remember any of it?"

Margaret's expression cooled quickly. "I remember all of it," she said, meeting Monica's eyes. "I'll tell you, but I don't want to talk about it in front of Millie. You all have to promise me you won't bring it up around her."

"We promise," I said, looking around to see that everyone nodded in agreement. Excitement filled me as I waited for her to begin. It felt like we were finally close to discovering the truth, not just about Margaret, but about everything.

She cleared her throat. "I was walking home from school the day I went missing, and a man in a black truck was pulled over near the sidewalk. He had the hood of the truck lifted like he was fixing it or something, and so I kept walking. My parents had lectured me all about 'stranger danger.' I knew not to talk to anyone I didn't know, but when I got near his truck, he said my name. I realized right away that I knew him, but I couldn't immediately decide why. I remember smiling at him and him saying how nice my smile was." She grimaced involuntarily, lost in her story.

"Who was he?" I asked.

She blinked. "Let me finish," she said. "And I promise I'll tell you everything." She sniffled as if she were congested and reached into a hidden pocket of her dress to pull out a wadded up tissue. She stuck it to the end of her nose, blowing and wiping aggressively before shoving it back into her pocket. "He asked if I needed a ride home, and I told him no because I wasn't far from my house. I could almost see it from where we stood. I've thought about that so much over the years...if I'd only walked a little faster, left a little earlier. If my mom had been outside, she may have heard me screaming." She sniffed again. "I was walking away from him when I heard the hood of his truck slam and his footsteps behind me. Dress shoes. They were different than the work boots my dad always wore. I remember thinking about how loud they clicked across the sidewalk. Before I knew what was happening, his hand was clamped over my mouth and we were in his truck." She shook her head. "It was broad daylight. I still don't know how no one managed to see us. This isn't New York City, you know? I screamed as loud as I could through his hand. I remember biting his skin, just praying that he'd drop me and I could run. My shoe fell off. It was a pink one with heels that lit up when you stepped. I thought, *hoped,* it would be like a bread crumb," she said softly, "like from the story of Hansel and Gretel." Her mouth twisted in what was either anger or sadness, I couldn't tell. "But no one found me. No one came for me. He took me to a cabin for a while. Then, eventually, he brought me back to his house. I was in…well, I think it was some sort of hidden room. Like a basement, but it locked from the outside."

I couldn't bear to ask what he'd done to her, but my mind wandered to the darkest corners it contained, causing me to shiver. She spoke softly, keeping her gaze locked on Millie so that she wouldn't have to meet ours. "I spent most of my life down there, I guess. More time than I've spent out so far. And…he wasn't always bad. I know what he did was bad, but he was kind to me. He brought me toys. He played games with me. Kept me fed and cleaned." She glanced at me but looked away quickly. "I'm not naïve. I *know* I was a victim. I know what he did was wrong. But I never felt like a victim. Maybe at first, I guess. I really missed my parents, at first. But eventually…it felt normal. I know it doesn't make sense."

"We all get making a horrible situation into something normal," Gray said. He moved to step forward, and she scooted further from him on the wooden step. He stopped moving, shoving his hands into his pockets and staring at the ground.

Margaret offered him a small apologetic smile out of one corner of her mouth. "Anyway, one day, he didn't make it down to visit me. That hadn't ever happened before. Even when I got really sick and couldn't do any of the things he wanted me to do on a normal day, he still came to check on me at least once a day after dinner when he'd bring me my food. He didn't come the next day either. Or the next. That was when I started to realize that something was really wrong. But what was I supposed to do, you know? I was stuck down there with no way out. He never left me much food or water, so I knew that I wouldn't make it long. But then…one day, I woke up and I heard people outside of my door. I'd never heard anyone out there—he either lived alone or no one came to that part of the house—so when I heard their voices, I really thought I was dreaming. But I kept hearing them. Over and over. And when I listened really closely…I could hear his voice."

"The man who kidnapped you?" I asked.

She shook her head. "No. My father's."

For a moment, I thought the response was sarcastic, but her serious expression told me I was mistaken. "Your father was in the house?"

"He was looking for me. At first, I wasn't sure what to do. I was afraid he'd be mad at me for everything that had happened, so I stayed quiet. When they found me, he stared at me like he didn't believe it was really me. I waited to see his expression, see how he felt about me, but it was hard to tell."

"I remember your parents after it happened," I told her. "They were devastated, Margaret. Everyone was."

She nodded sadly. "I know, but it just felt wrong to me. Like…he was expecting something different. He was expecting his little girl to walk out of that room, and I was far from it. We didn't know how to live together anymore. He and my mom had gotten divorced, and it was like, even though he'd spent so much time searching for me, once he found me…I don't know, maybe the excitement was over?"

"But how did they find you?" Cole asked.

"Well, it's complicated. You said you've heard the rumors of a curse in Fallen Oaks?" she asked.

I was half tempted to roll my eyes, finally thinking we'd

gotten away from the curse folklore and on to something I could hold onto. Instead, I nodded as I waited for her to tell us all about the fabled curse.

"Well, there are a few different stories, but the gist is that, supposedly, a group of people cursed the land they built Gerbera on because the people who founded our town murdered a bunch of innocent people…" She nodded slowly, watching as we nodded in confirmation that we knew what she was talking about. "Well, according to my dad, it was all a lie."

Now, *that,* I hadn't been expecting. I sucked in a sharp breath and furrowed my brow. "What do you mean?"

"He wasn't supposed to tell me anything, but I wanted to know what had happened. I needed to know." She leaned her head over to check on Millie, who was still content chasing her butterfly—or maybe it was a new one—through the yard. "I wish I'd never asked."

"What did he tell you, Margaret? Does it have something to do with our parents or the curse…or you?"

"Everything. They're all tied together," she said finally, letting out a huff of air. "Just like we are now."

I cocked my head to the side, waiting for her to explain.

"You guys aren't the only ones to make it out of Gerbera alive that day. I'm the sixth survivor."

CHAPTER EIGHTEEN

October 4th

"The man who kept you prisoner lived in our subdivision?" I asked, my stomach roiling with the realization. "You were right under our noses, being held prisoner, and none of us knew it?"

She nodded. "You were all kids, too. No one could've known, and no one was to blame except the people involved in my kidnapping."

"People?" A cold chill ran down my spine, and I couldn't help but to run my hands over my arms to warm them. "I thought it was just one man."

"One man kidnapped me. Held me prisoner for his own sick gains, yes. But they were all involved. They were all to blame."

I almost hated to ask, but Cole took the lead on the next question on all of our minds. "They?"

"Everyone who lived in Gerbera," Margaret said. "Your families."

"No!" Cassie cried out, her voice full of pain. I reached for her arm, caressing it gently, though my brain was screaming the same thing. It wasn't possible. Maybe I couldn't be sure about everyone other than our parents, but I knew our parents. I knew what they were capable of and what they weren't…didn't I?

"You aren't seriously expecting us to believe our parents had anything to do with kidnapping you?" Gray asked with a scoff. "No way. No *way.* What could they have possibly gotten out of that? It's not like your family had any money."

"They didn't want money," she said sharply, standing from the porch step and brushing off her bottom before she spoke again. "They weren't directly involved in the kidnapping, but they were why I was taken. You see, the fact that your families all lived in Gerbera was no coincidence. I'm not sure if you guys know this, but even before they lived in the same neighborhood, all of the families worked together at the chemical plant in Tarson. That's why they lived so close. At one point, they were all inseparable."

I nodded. I vaguely remembered my mom mentioning her years at a factory before she moved into the CFO position she'd worked during the early years of my childhood. The factory had been where she met my dad. I had no idea she'd worked alongside any of our neighbors. But, then again, we'd never talked much about it. It seemed like such a small part of her past, a meaningless first job on the way to something better.

"It's a small town, Margaret. Our parents working at the same place or even being friends back in the day doesn't mean anything," Cole said, his tone annoyed. He was right, although I would've never approached the subject like that.

We needed to keep her happy if we ever hoped to get the rest of the story.

"It's weird, though. A pretty big coincidence for sure," I agreed. "My mom never mentioned being friends with any of them."

"But they didn't just *work* together, you guys. They weren't *just* best friends. They committed a crime together." She paused as she said the words, letting them sink in. An audible gasp was heard from each of us and my head shook without volition. *No.* I knew my parents. They weren't criminals.

"What the hell are you talking about?" Gray demanded, stepping a bit closer. I watched the way his forehead wrinkled as he grew agitated. Of the two men in our group, there was no doubt that Gray was the more soft spoken and reserved, but when he did speak, there was much more power to his words. I had to appreciate that about him.

"Dave told me," she said firmly. "He told me about everything."

"Dave?" I asked, because there was only one *Dave* I could think of that had lived in our subdivision. "You're saying... Dave Thompson was the man who kidnapped you?"

Cole's gaze shot to me, followed closely by Gray's, Monica's, and Cassie's. "Mr. Thompson?" Cassie asked with a horrified expression on her face.

"The superintendent?" Cole asked, equally disgusted.

Margaret gave a quick nod. "He worked with them. He *said* he was their boss, but he was lying about that."

"If he was lying about that, how do you know he wasn't lying about the rest of it?" Gray asked.

She looked at him, her dark eyes narrowing. "He was the

only person I saw for nine years. I had nothing better to do than learn how to read him."

"What did they do?" I asked, wondering why we were still arguing about anything other than that. I needed to know.

She looked back at me, glancing down at her hands held clasped in her lap and then back up at me. "They killed the first Daisy."

"Wait, what?" I asked, staring at her with utter confusion. "What first Daisy? What does that mean?"

"Your parents killed a little girl named Daisy Thompson years ago. It's why all of this happened." She said the words, though they didn't seem to be registering with my brain. I stared at the ground, trying desperately to understand what we were being told. I didn't want to believe it. I couldn't. As much as I'd believed that there must be *some* reason for all of this, I couldn't believe that could be the reason. My parents didn't kill anyone. They weren't monsters.

"No," Cole argued, his chest puffed up as if he were preparing to fight. "No way. You're a fucking liar."

"I'm not lying!" Margaret said, standing up from the step. "It's the truth. Honestly it is. And if you want to hear the rest of it, you'd better not accuse me of lying anymore." It was obvious he'd hit a nerve with her, and with tensions running high all around, I tried to find a way to push forward. I felt the anxiety growing in my body, like waves of panic washing through me. I needed to breathe, or I was going to end up having a panic attack, and then I'd be of no use to anyone. I shoved my hands in my pockets, pinching my thighs so I could focus on something else. Pain seemed to bring me back from the brink every time.

"Tell us the story, Margaret," I begged, unable to look at her. I hoped the others wouldn't notice how my voice shook.

"Tell us everything you know, and I promise we'll believe you."

I was as close as I'd ever been to knowing the truth about my parents' deaths—and their lives, apparently—and I couldn't let anything stand in the way of that.

"Dave had a daughter really young. He was only fifteen when she was born and the girl's mom ran away. He was devastated at the time, too young to be raising a kid on his own, but he didn't see any way out. He named her Daisy. She would've been a few years older than us, if she'd lived." She paused for what seemed like a dramatic effect, but I realized she was checking to make sure Millie hadn't left the yard before she continued. "The chemical plant your parents worked for was supposed to haul off the chemicals that they couldn't use. There was some sort of procedure for getting rid of them, though I'm not sure what all was supposed to be done, but your parents decided to cut corners. The way Dave told it, they cut a few dollars here and there by illegally dumping the chemicals in the woods behind the factory. He lived close by and caught them doing it, but when he tried to report them, he was fired. He had papers and documentation for the disposal, and he could prove they were all altered. All of it. But the company didn't care. They wouldn't listen to him. Wouldn't take him seriously." I could sense her agitation as she told the story, and I wondered just how many times she'd heard it. Enough that she'd grown angry herself? Or was she angry because of all the harm it had caused her? "Daisy was home with Dave's mom one day while he was at a job interview. He said he wasn't gone but maybe two hours. When he got home, she was dead."

"How?" Cole asked. "What does any of that have to do

with our parents? They killed his daughter because he was trying to get them into trouble? I don't buy it—"

"Let her finish," I demanded.

"Daisy had been swimming in a pond behind Dave's house. It was contaminated with all of the chemicals they'd dumped. He had an autopsy run that proved she was exposed to several of the chemicals that plant manufactured." She shook her head. "But it still wasn't enough. Nothing he did was enough and Daisy was just…gone."

"That's horrible," Cassie said from behind me. When I looked her way, her pale fingers covered her mouth. "I can't believe they could do something so…evil."

They didn't know, I wanted to say, to defend them, more for Cassie's sake than theirs. I couldn't make the words form, desperate as I was. How could I justify such actions? More than that, how could I justify the fact that I still loved them just the same?

"When your parents moved into the subdivision, they named it Gerbera. Dave always believed they were mocking him."

"Maybe it was their way of apologizing," Monica said. "Like a tribute. Or a dedication."

It was a nice thought, and I couldn't help hoping it were true. "He didn't see it that way. Dave moved into the subdivision to make sure they never forgot what they'd done," Margaret said, her voice low as Millie grew closer to us in her search for the elusive butterfly. "He said as long as he lived, he would make sure to be a constant reminder that his daughter had mattered. And then, when he saw me…I think he thought I could be a replacement for her. We looked similar enough. Especially then, my hair was darker. He wanted me to ease his pain, but I couldn't. Eventually, I wanted to just as badly as he did, but it was impossible. There were nights that he'd tuck me into bed and read me a story with tears in his eyes. Even the good moments were so filled with memories of Daisy that he couldn't enjoy them. I tried to be a good replacement for her, honestly I did, but I wasn't enough. There were days he was so depressed he could hardly carry a conversation."

"Margaret, it wasn't your place to help him," I said, my voice barely above a whisper. "You were just a child." It was a phrase my therapist had said to me over and over, but it seemed appropriate there.

"Toward the end," she went on, "I think he regretted his decision. The fact that I was a detective's daughter, though it was sheer dumb luck on his part, had made things incredibly difficult. Sometimes, I think maybe he'd have given me back if he weren't so terrified that my dad would've caught him. By that point, I knew him so well. To give me back, even if I'd tried to keep his identity a secret, would've been a death sentence. I just...knew too much."

As I listened to her story, I couldn't help thinking of the many times I'd gone out to play in my yard and spotted Mr. Thompson walking around our cul-de-sac or staring at me from one of his darkened windows as I played in the street with my friends. How close had I been to being the one he'd taken? Granted, me with my brown hair and stockier build than Margaret or Daisy, I wouldn't have been the obvious choice, but still. How many times had I played outside, just feet from his house, while he was holding a girl my own age hostage? It sent shivers down my spine.

"So, it was Mr. Thompson, then? He's the one who... killed them? Because of what happened to Daisy?" I nodded as I spoke, just waiting for her to fill in the blanks. It still didn't explain who had helped him. There were many masked men that night, while Mr. Thompson seemed like quite the loner.

"No," she said quickly, a hand in the air as if to pluck the thought straight from existence. "No, of course not."

I reeled back. "*No?* I don't understand. If not Mr. Thompson, then who?"

She squinted her eyes shut, bracing herself as she spoke the words that caused her visible pain. "My dad."

"What?" the five of us asked in unison.

She took a deep breath, refusing to meet any of our eyes as she gave us the final piece of the puzzle. "My father, Larry Gold. The detective. He's the one who killed your parents."

"I don't understand," Gray said. "Why? Why would he do that?"

"Did he know what had happened to you? That it was our parents' fault?" Monica asked.

It wasn't the worst guess, but Margaret shook her head. "No. My father was looking for me, that's the only reason. He came to Gerbera because he'd gotten an anonymous tip that I was being held there, but he didn't know for sure which house. He tried to come around and ask questions, even asked to search people's houses, but he didn't have warrants. People weren't kind to him about it, as you can imagine, but my dad isn't one to give up. He wasn't going to stop looking for me. It had been years since I'd gone missing, and most people believed I was dead." She shrugged. "I can't blame them for that. But I told you about the day he found me. Dave had left the house and he never came back. I remember hearing noises upstairs. Gunshots. People screaming. I stayed in the basement. It was the only home I'd known for most of my life. When my dad opened that basement door, it was the last thing I ever thought I'd see. *He* was the last person I ever thought I'd see. But there he was." She brushed a tear from her eye quickly. "He never admitted to killing your parents. He wouldn't, but he was smiling when he told me that a few days after he'd asked to search their homes and been turned away, they were all dead, and he was allowed to search anywhere he liked. I knew the truth. I knew what he'd done."

It was a sick sort of irony that Mr. Thompson had eventually ended our parents' lives like he'd wanted, though his was ended as well.

"So your father killed all those people, saved you, and now you two just get to live happily ever after while the rest of us have to suffer?" Cole asked, his fists balled at his sides. "How the fuck is that fair?"

Her voice was filled with venom when she responded, her cheeks burning red. "Does it look like I'm living happily ever after?" she demanded, gesturing around the rickety farm house. "I haven't seen my dad in years. I told you I wasn't the little girl he thought he'd find in that basement. I had Millie by that point. I'd grown up. He wanted his little girl back, but I'll never be her again. I couldn't stay with him knowing that I wasn't what he expected anymore. We didn't work together…it was like we were two pieces of a puzzle that just didn't fit. So, no, I don't get a happily ever after here. Neither does my dad. Or Dave. Or any of you, for that matter. I don't think any of us got a happily ever after in this story. Now, if you'll excuse me, I need to get Millie inside to wash up. I think it's time for you all to leave."

Without waiting for us to say another word, she called for her daughter, waving her up onto the porch and turning away from us. That was that.

CHAPTER NINETEEN

October 4th

We sat in the hotel room that night in Raleigh, just a half-hour drive from Fallen Oaks, trying desperately to process everything we'd learned that day. Gray was reclining in the maroon, upholstered chair next to the bed, one foot underneath him as he stuck another hand in the bag of chips shoved in between him and the arm of the chair.

Monica sat awkwardly on the edge of the bed closest to me, scrolling through her phone. Occasionally, she'd tuck a strand of her dark hair behind her ears and then, a few seconds later, untuck it again. I was beginning to think it was a nervous tic.

Cassie lay in the second bed, her knees drawn into her chest as she slept—or at least, pretended to sleep. I wasn't sure how anyone could've slept after the news we'd received, but she was yawning before we were able to check in, and it honestly gave me a bit of relief to know that she was sleeping peacefully while I tapped my foot on the ground nervously in the desk chair at the end of the bed. I couldn't seem to pull my eyes from the door, watching anxiously as we waited for Cole to return with our food. He'd said he was starving and, truth be told, we all were, but no one else volunteered to pick up the food.

I sucked in a deep breath, trying to keep the panic attack I could feel coming on at bay. My therapist had taught me tapping techniques meant to combat my anxiety during one of my first sessions, and for a while, I used them daily. It had been some time since I'd had to break them out, but I thought learning your parents had been murderers certainly warranted that.

Speaking of, I picked up my phone, sending a quick text to my therapist to let him know that I wouldn't make it in for my Monday session, that I was back home and doing okay. It was a lie, and he was sure to see straight through it, but what choice did I have? I also sent a text to my boss, who much preferred phone calls as he'd made it abundantly clear, to let him know that I wouldn't be in on Monday. I told him I'd had a family emergency, which I supposed wasn't a total lie.

After the texts were sent, I placed the phone back on the cheap, brown desk in front of me, flipping through the logo-covered notepad in front of me. A small comment card lay beside the notepad, asking me how my stay had been. I couldn't help but roll my eyes, thinking of the many people who'd flocked in and out of those rooms—happy smiles on their faces as they envisioned the fun they'd have on their family vacation. How many people had experienced the best day of their lives in the very spot where I was currently experiencing the worst?

The handle on the door jingled, and I heard the automatic lock open as Cole swiped the keycard, allowing him access to us. He propped the door open with his foot, balancing a drink tray in one hand, a brown paper bag in the other, and one more drink between his forearms and chin. I stood, moving to rush forward to help, but Monica beat me to it. Together, they set our dinner down, and my mouth began to salivate. There was no denying how hungry I'd become without realizing it.

I looked over at Cassie, wondering whether to wake her but deciding to be sure to save her a few of the tacos in the bag.

"I got twenty total, so four each. And everyone just got a Coke. Hope that's okay."

"It's fine, Cole," I answered for the group, not allowing them a chance to complain when not one of them—myself included—had offered to go in his place. "Thank you for going to get it."

"No problem," he assured me, digging into the bag with both hands and pulling out four tightly-wrapped tacos. He sank onto the edge of the bed Cassie was sleeping on, unwrapping one and shoving it into his mouth. "I'm starving," he said with a mouthful of food. I opened the wrapper that protected my taco, taking a bite of the lukewarm dinner.

"So," Gray's voice filled the silence, "what are we going to do?" I turned my head to look at him. I'd hoped to go longer without discussing our impending problems, but I knew that wasn't likely.

"I don't know if we should believe her," I said finally, because no one else had spoken. "None of us really know her."

"Plus, she was held prisoner, basically, for all those years," Cole said, picking at his taco. "Maybe it makes me a dick to say this, but that has to mess with your head. Who knows if she's even...ya know, sane, or whatever."

His words were cold, but could I deny their validity? We didn't know Margaret. Not really. Why should we believe anything she'd said?

"I overheard my parents arguing once," Gray said, staring at the floor but finally looking up to meet our eyes, "about Mr. Thompson. When he moved in. I was little, ya know, so I don't remember much, but that's stuck in my head on replay ever since we talked to Margaret. They were mad about him being there. I remember my dad asking what my mom thought he was doing living down the street from us. I didn't know what the issue was, and I never heard them talk about it again. But now I keep thinking, what if she was telling the truth?"

Cole shook his head. "My parents wouldn't have killed a kid. There's no way. They were good people. They were foster parents to dozens of kids, for God's sake. They loved children! They couldn't have killed anyone, let alone a child."

"We all think that," I argued. "But we don't know." His face grew angry as I spoke, but I looked at Cassie lying on the bed to avert my attention. "We don't really know them like we think we did. They had secrets, just like everyone else. It wasn't like they intentionally killed anyone. It was an accident, Margaret even said that. They were cutting a few corners to save a bit of money. It's not like that's unheard of."

"So, we need to look into Daisy's death, then. That's the only way to know," Monica said.

"We still wouldn't know, though," Cole argued. "Even if she died the way Margaret said, that doesn't prove that our parents had anything to do with it."

"And if they did? Did they deserve to die like that?

Slaughtered like animals?" Gray asked, his voice shaking with anger.

"Of course not," I said. "No one deserved to die that way." Memories flashed back to me from that night, and I closed my eyes, shaking my head free of them.

"But, in the end, *if* we choose to believe her…they died because of something they did, right?" Cole asked. "That's what we're saying. Objectively, an outsider would say they deserved it."

"We aren't outsiders," I told him quickly. "And we don't have to look at it like that. Even if they did what Margaret said, even if they did something that horrible, they were still our parents. For all we know, they spent their lives trying to make up for that one horrible deed. My parents were amazing parents, and I won't choose to remember them any other way."

"Me either," Monica agreed. "My dad could make me laugh no matter how mad I was." She chuckled at the mere thought.

"My mom made homemade chicken noodle soup when I had a cold," Gray told us. "She hated it. Hated making the noodles. So, it was only when I was sick."

Cole smiled. "My dad could throw a mean spiral."

"Everyone has a bit of darkness and a bit of light inside of them," I recited, remembering the words my therapist had told me. "It's the part that you choose to act on that matters. If our parents messed up, it was when they were…what, our age now? And they spent another fifteen or so years making up for it."

"We need to tell someone what we know. All of it. They need to make sure that Margaret's dad goes down for what he did to our families." This time, it was Monica who spoke with confidence. She was staring directly at me, waiting for me to agree with her.

"Who would we tell?" I challenged. "If Margaret's father was in on it as Lieutenant, there's a very real chance the police already know and are part of the cover up. He didn't act alone, after all."

"You really think the police would do something so horrible?" Cole asked, pulling his phone out of his pocket and staring at the screen.

I shrugged. "Up until a few hours ago," Gray said, "I didn't believe our parents could do something so horrible."

"So, what then? We just give up? And, if the police *are* in on it, are they the ones who wrote us the notes?" Monica asked. Her voice squeaked with her final question. "Are they trying to kill us?"

"They can't be," Cole said. "That makes no sense. They've had too many opportunities. Why not do it when we first got to town? Before anyone even knew we were here?"

"Cole's right," I said. "It doesn't add up. And why the 'Daisy' notes?"

"To tie it to Mr. Thompson," Gray answered.

"Or Gerbera in general," Monica said. "To make sure we knew what they were talking about."

"How could we not?" I whined. I was getting a stress headache from all the worry and fear I'd carried over the past few days, even more than usual, which I hadn't believed possible at one point.

"I don't know," Monica said. She stared at the phone she'd laid on the comforter. "But honestly I'm ready to go home and forget about it all. I'm so tired of thinking about all of this."

"Go home?" Gray exclaimed, standing up in shock. "We can't just *go home*."

"I don't know how your jobs work, but at mine, if I don't show up, I don't get paid. I can't afford to keep traipsing all over Fallen Oaks in search of answers that we'll probably never get anyway. This is the third text from my boss," she said, gesturing toward her phone, "that I've gotten since I called in yesterday. We have to go back."

"But we could still be in danger," I said. "Wasn't that the whole reason you all wanted to come here?"

"And we're still in danger here," Monica argued. "Probably even more so than before because we can't seem to find any answers, and we just keep digging further and further into this mess." She flopped back onto the bed dramatically, causing Cassie to stir in her sleep. "All I know is that, no matter what we find out, we still have to go back to our regular lives and cope with all of this *mess*. I, for one, have no desire to dig up anything else that might further uproot the small sense of peace I had in my life." She let out an exasperated sigh, seemingly done with her rant, and closed her eyes.

I looked to Cole and then to Gray before nodding. "She's right," I said. Monica's eyes popped open, obviously expecting me to disagree. "Cassie needs to get back to school, and I have work. We all have lives that have been disrupted enough by whatever it is that our parents were—or weren't—involved in. We need to go home and try to move on from all of this once and for all."

"Can you do that?" Gray asked, his dark eyes narrowing at mine.

"What choice do we have?" I asked, the only words I could muster.

I AWOKE TO A STRANGE NOISE. My eyes popped open instantaneously, and I stared around the dark room. The only hint of light came in the form of a blue glow from the alarm clock across the room. The time was projected on the ceiling from its top, letting me know it was just past two in the morning.

I sat up, staring across the bed. Cassie was beside me and Monica lay next to her. I could vaguely make out the shape of Gray in the chair next to the bed. I looked to my left and flipped on the bedside lamp, expecting to see Cole in the opposite bed, but instead, the covers were thrown back and he was nowhere in sight.

I cocked my ear toward the ceiling, listening carefully for the sound as it came again. Whimpering.

Breathing.

What was that?

I pulled my legs from the covers, looking around to see what I could use for a weapon if I needed one. I settled on the television remote, though I knew it would do me little good, and walked toward the source of the sound. My feet slid across the rough carpet quietly as I approached the bathroom door. I pressed my ear to the wood and listened.

There it was again, quiet whimpering. "Cole?" I whispered his name, my heart thudding so loudly in my ears I was sure I wouldn't hear it if he answered.

The noise stopped instantly, and I heard him take a deep breath before answering with a distraught voice. "Just a second."

"Are you okay?" I asked. "It sounds like you're crying."

"I'm fine," he snapped.

I took a step back, refusing to let myself get angry over

the response. "Are you sure? Can you let me in?" If he could interrupt me in the shower, I could interrupt whatever he was—I stopped, heat flooding to my cheeks. What exactly was I interrupting? The thought of Cole in the bathroom doing anything other than *using the bathroom* was enough to cause my heart to pound and my ears to burn. "S-sorry," I apologized, stepping back so quickly I nearly tripped over my feet.

"What's going on?" Cassie's sleepy voice asked from across the room. I looked over to see her rubbing her eyes and stretching in bed. Beside her, Monica rolled over, staring at me and then Cassie in confusion.

"What's happening?" she asked.

Gray began to stir as I stood mortified between Cole doing whatever he was doing and everyone else discovering what he was doing. Why the hell was I trying to cover for the perv, I wondered as the first excuse I could think of flew out of my mouth. "Sorry, guys. I needed to use the bathroom. I didn't mean to wake you."

"Why do you look like you've seen a ghost?" Cassie asked, not buying my lie at all.

As I fumbled through the mess of words and excuses and lies in my head, I felt relief as the bathroom door opened behind me. I turned around, prepared to apologize profusely, but gasped instead. "What happened?" I asked, hearing the sounds of the others gasping behind me.

Cole walked from the bathroom with a towel wrapped around his hand. The white had been dyed a crimson red and his bloodshot eyes told the tale of the pain that he was carrying.

"Are you okay?" Monica asked.

Cole walked past me, nodding only slightly as he sank

into the bed. "Sorry to wake you up. I'm fine." He rolled over in bed, covering himself with his one good hand.

"You're obviously not fine," I said, moving toward him. I pulled the covers back away from his chest and reached for his hand without allowing myself to worry about whether I should. "What did you do?"

"It's nothing," he said, pulling his hand from my grasp.

"That looks really bad, man," Gray said, standing from his chair and making his way toward us. "You may need stitches."

We couldn't see the wound, but I couldn't help agreeing with Gray. His hand had to be a mess if the amount of blood lost was any indication. "Did you fall?" I asked. "Is it broken?"

"I said it's nothing, okay?" Cole retorted, causing me to jump. His words were harsh, his tone harsher. "Just leave me alone, all of you."

"Fine," I said finally, my feelings hurt by his callousness. "I was only trying to help."

"Dick move, dude," Gray said, obviously just as hurt. He stood from the edge of the bed where he was resting and flipped off the lamp light before making his way back to the chair. I flopped onto the bed and pulled the covers back up over my arms, trying to rid them of the goosebumps they were sporting.

I closed my eyes, opening them to stare at the blue lights on the ceiling and watch as the time changed minute by minute. It wouldn't be long until we were up and ready to head home.

Home. The thought exhilarated and terrified me all at once. I was ready to be back to normal, just Cassie and I. It seemed like a lifetime ago that things had been that way, when in reality it was just a few days. I couldn't believe how much had changed in such a short amount of time.

"I get angry sometimes." His soft voice carried across the room with a sense of uncertainty. I wasn't sure I'd heard it at first, but after a moment, he spoke again. "I don't know why. Most of the time I can control it, but sometimes I can't."

I stared at the ceiling. "Have you…always been that way?"

"No," he answered, his voice distorted by anger or tears, I couldn't tell.

"Just since—"

"Since we lost them, yeah."

I nodded, not looking his way. I felt a cool tear form in the corner of my eye before running down the side of my face and into my hair. "My panic attacks are like that. I can't control them, and they come out of nowhere sometimes."

"I didn't realize you had…"

"Severe anxiety," I filled in the blank he'd left open. "And depression. And PTSD. And OCD. I'm a walking billboard for mental illness."

"You're doing better," Cassie said, reaching out her hand to touch my arm.

I nodded. "I am, but it's not ever going to go away completely."

"Sometimes I think it would've been better if we'd all just died when they did," Monica admitted, her voice broken up by a sob. "Things would've been easier."

Try as I might to find a reason to argue with her, I couldn't. I wouldn't deny I'd had those thoughts myself on more than one occasion. Except for Cassie. I was doing everything in my power to make sure she had a life worth living.

"Every time I hear a car backfire, or a door slam just loud

enough, I feel like I could be physically sick." It was Gray's voice that carried across the darkness that time.

"I still dream about them. About that day," Cassie said. It was the first time she'd told me that, and my heart broke at her confession. "I can remember her scream so clearly." I squeezed her hand, running my thumb over her knuckles.

"I get so sick of people complaining about normal things, ya know?" Cole asked. "Like, you're at the store and some old lady's complaining about her coupon not working or you hear someone at a restaurant saying the service isn't fast enough. I just…I want to shake them. I sound crazy, I know, but I get this urge to just grab them and scream at them. Don't they know what a bad day truly is?" He spoke through a sarcastic laugh. "My fucking food had a hair in it, *fuck you.* You could die. Any moment." He snapped his fingers. "Just like that it could be over."

"I think about death every day," I admitted. "It's almost all I think about."

"People think I'm crazy," Monica said. "Or damaged. I mean, I guess I am, but I'm doing all I can to get better."

"Do you think that's possible?" Gray asked. "For any of us to get better? After all we've seen?"

No. The answer in my head was incredibly clear, but I couldn't bring myself to say it. "I don't know," I said finally, "but I hope so."

"Cole, are you sure your hand is okay?" Monica asked after the room grew quiet again.

He chuckled. "I'm fine. Not the first time I've busted a knuckle or two, and it won't be the last."

"What did you punch?" Gray asked.

"The counter," he said. "I hit the edge by mistake."

"Ouch," Cassie said.

"Yeah, you can say that again," he said.

Again, we grew silent, and I thought for a moment that we must all be going back to sleep. As I felt myself dozing off, I heard Cole's voice again. "Do you ever wonder what life would've been like if they'd lived? Like, what our lives should've been."

I shook my head, starting to answer, but Gray beat me to it. "All the time. I could've gone to college at UNC, just like my dad. I'd be a lawyer right now."

"I was gonna play football," Cole said. "I could've gone pro."

"I wanted to be a mom," Monica said, her wish causing more tears to flood my vision. "I didn't need anything special, just…that. Just a baby and a husband."

How had our lives been derailed so much that even the simplest of dreams were now impossible? I tried to remember what my own dreams had been, but I couldn't. Too much had changed. I hadn't allowed myself to dream of possibilities in so long it seemed impossible at that point.

"I wanted to be a doctor, like my dad," Cassie said. Add that to the long list of things I never knew about my sister. She never failed to amaze me.

"You could still do that, Cass," I told her. "You still have your whole life ahead of you."

"No medical school is going to accept a girl who had to repeat a grade in elementary school, even if it's because her parents died."

"You don't know that," I argued, though I had no idea how college admissions worked.

"Besides that, we can't afford for me to go to medical school."

"We would find a way," I promised her. "Don't give up just yet, okay?"

She laughed under her breath as if I were joking, though I wanted desperately not to be.

"I wish we could see them again," Monica broke the silence again. "Just once, you know?"

"What would you say to them?" I asked, yawning loudly.

"I'd say that I miss them." she said. "And that I'm trying to make them proud even though I struggle." She sniffled. "And I'd say that I'm sorry and that I forgive them. If what Margaret said is true, I still forgive them."

"I'd say that I hope I make them proud," Cassie said. "And that I'll never forget them."

"I'd tell them thank you for everything," Cole said. "And I'm sorry for being such a little shit sometimes."

We laughed along with him, and I wiped a tear from my eyes. "I'd tell them we're still here. Still fighting to be here even though it's hard."

"I'd tell them I'm sorry I fought with them the night before they died. It was stupid, the party wasn't worth it, and I've never forgiven myself for the things I said to them...the last things I ever said to them." Gray's voice was choked up, much like the rest of ours, though we all tried to conceal our tears.

"At least you can remember the last thing you said to them," Cole said. "I don't remember what I said to my parents last."

"Me either," Monica said. "I wish I did, but I don't. You're supposed to remember your last words, you know, but what happens when you don't know they're your last until it's too late?"

"My therapist says you should write letters to the people

you love in case you die unexpectedly. That way you can say everything you needed to say and you have time to prepare it," I said.

"You see a therapist?" Cole asked. Of course that was the only thing he'd gotten out of that sentence.

"I do." It had taken me a long time to not feel ashamed to admit that. "He's probably saved my life more times than I can count."

"I should probably find someone to talk to," he whispered, much to my surprise.

"I'm sure Doctor Porter could recommend someone for you."

"I may take you up on that once we get home," he said, stifling a yawn.

"I wish our parents had written us one of those letters," Cassie said. "I wish we'd been able to hear the truth from them rather than a stranger."

"Me too," I agreed. As my eyes closed slowly, darkness filling my mind, I couldn't help thinking about how true that was, and how much trouble the truth could've saved us all.

"Truth is relative," Gray whispered. It was the last thing I heard before I drifted off to sleep.

Later that morning, we awoke and gathered our bags together. No one spoke of our early morning conversation, for which I was incredibly grateful. None of us had packed much, just preparing for the one day, so it didn't take long to get ready. I ran a quick brush through my hair before handing it off to Cassie to do the same. She hadn't said much since she'd woken up—hadn't said much since we'd spoken to Margaret, honestly—but she nodded when I met her eyes as if to assure me she was okay.

Were any of us okay, though? How could we be with what we'd uncovered? Cole paced by the door with the room key in his hand. "Are you guys about ready?" he asked for the third time. Something I was learning about Cole was that he was a very early riser. By the time I'd managed to rouse myself from sleep, sometime around seven, he'd already been down to the gym for a workout and had himself two cups of coffee. I tried my hardest not to be bothered by how thrown off my routine was since we'd been on the road, but the fact that my cuticles had been chewed to bits said otherwise. I was ready to be home. Ready to get back to the strange existence I knew as normal.

I'd sent a text to my boss that morning to let him know I'd be home and back to work the next day. We just had to make it through the actual anniversary without thinking too much about it and get back to our lives. Somehow that day, the fated anniversary, felt like a milestone. Like if we could just make it to the end of the day, everything would somehow be better. Safer. It was the obstacle we had to conquer.

We filed toward the door, Cassie just behind me, Gray in front, and Monica pulling up the rear as Cole opened the door. Cassie shoved the hairbrush in the front of our bag and, together, we walked from the room and down the musty hotel hallway on our way to check out.

Before we arrived at the front desk, I saw a silhouette that caused the blood to drain from my face. Detective McDuffy stood inside the glass double doors of the hotel, talking to a man I didn't recognize. "Guys," I said, realizing that none of them had noticed him just yet.

Their eyes followed mine just in time for the second set of doors to open and allow McDuffy to pass through. We were frozen in place as his eyes trailed across the lobby before landing on us. He raised a hand, waving casually at us before heading our way. Every part of me screamed that we should bolt. That we should run as fast and as far as we could before he had the chance to stop us. But as I stood in the crowded lobby, blood running ice cold through my body and contemplating all of my options—of which there seemed to be very few—the detective walked straight toward us and stopped dead in front of me with a determined glare.

"I thought that was you. What are you all doing here?" he asked, looking at Cole suddenly.

"We were just leaving," I answered, my voice full of venom. I looked over the messy, salt and pepper hair of the detective, wondering what he could be doing there. What were the chances of him being so many miles outside of Fallen Oaks? And at the exact same hotel we'd chosen to stay? There was no way it was a coincidence. But what did he want?

He nodded, his full lips pressed into a thin line behind the scruff of his facial hair. "I take it everything's okay, then? Nothing else out of the ordinary?"

I shook my head. "Everything's fine. Thank you, Detective. We'd better go."

To my surprise, he didn't try to stop us as we walked away, though I felt his gaze follow us to the desk to turn in our room key and then out the double doors toward my car. We climbed into the car silently, and I started it up. In the rearview, I saw the detective standing just outside the door, his head turning with the car as we made our way across the parking lot, pulling out swiftly in front of a red truck that had to slam on its brakes to avoid hitting us. I offered up a mental apology, though it meant nothing to anyone but me, and pressed down on the accelerator, speeding through the yellow light in an attempt to get as far from the hotel as possible.

Once we'd made it through the light, I checked the rearview for the detective's car—or what I thought it must look like—and let out a sigh of relief when I saw nothing to cause alarm.

"What do you think he was doing there?" Cassie asked, looking back over her shoulder from the backseat. She was wedged in between Gray and Monica.

"I don't know," I said honestly, pressing down on the brake at the next red light. "But I don't plan to stick around to find out."

"He had no reason to be in Raleigh," Cole said. "Fallen Oaks cops can't have any jurisdiction here, can they?"

"I wouldn't think so," I said, shaking my head.

"Maybe he was just on vacation," Cassie said. "It's possible, isn't it?"

"It's possible," I agreed, though I knew none of us truly believed that could be the reason for his untimely appearance.

"What if they're following us?" Monica asked.

"I'm keeping an eye out," I promised, moving to the right lane to take a turn at the next light for good measure. "I don't think he got into his car in time to see where we were headed."

"But he knows where we all live. Because we gave him the letters," Monica said, her voice quivering with fear as her wide eyes met mine in the rearview mirror. "He could find us whether we're here or there."

"She's right," Cole agreed, looking at me for guidance. So much had changed in such a short time. Once the most bull-headed and egotistical of our group, he now seemed to have relinquished his role of being the most knowledgeable, seeking my approval whenever he could get it. I didn't want to lead. I didn't want to make decisions. But somehow, the role had been given to me.

"We have to make a choice and stick with it, guys. No matter where we go, there's a chance that whoever wants us could find us. Even if we move and never return to our apartments and houses, there's still a chance we'd be found."

"Well, that's reassuring," Gray said with a scoff. I rolled my eyes, though he couldn't see me.

"I'm not going to promise you that everything's going to be okay," I said, making a sharp right at the next street as the light switched from green to yellow. I was sure, at that point, that we weren't being followed. "I have no way to know that, even if I wanted to. I'm just as scared as all of you. But we made it to the anniversary. And we made it past the detective without incident. For all we know, we'll just keep making it through the hard days until it gets a little easier. That's what we've been doing all along, isn't it?"

I'd spoken too soon. As I glanced up at the sudden change in my rearview mirror, I spotted the unmarked black car that warned me danger was near. Coming from the dash and the front of his grill, blue and white lights shone, commanding that I stop. I toyed with the idea of gunning it. We were on a quiet street, away from metropolitan downtown, and there were no witnesses around—no one to see it if a crime were committed by us or against us. Unfortunately, that last one was the one I was worried about more.

"You can't stop," Cole warned, grabbing ahold of the wheel to keep me from pulling to the side of the street.

"What choice do I have?" I asked, already letting my foot off the gas. "I can't outrun him."

"He's got us if you stop. We have no way to protect ourselves," Monica cried, her voice cracking from the backseat. I felt a lump swell in my throat as I met Cassie's tear filled eyes.

"I don't have a choice," I said, begging her to understand. "We have to stop."

She nodded, though no one else seemed to agree. "I'm not a good enough driver to outrun him." I was willing to admit my faults.

"Should I call nine one one?" Cole asked. "Isn't that a thing? I can have them on the line when he gets up here."

I couldn't answer the question; no real answer seemed to be enough. How could we attempt to explain this to an unwitting dispatcher? My entire body shook violently as adrenaline coursed through me with a strength I hadn't known possible. I seemed to have no control over my limbs as they flopped wildly. I pinned my arms in between my legs, chewing on my bottom lip until I tasted blood. I watched his car come to a stop behind mine and saw him climb from the car almost in an instant. That seemed strange to me. The few times I'd gotten pulled over before, it had taken a moment for the officer to approach my car, but there he was, headed toward me immediately. He held his hands up, no gun in them as he made his way down the quiet street. The sunglasses masked his eyes, but he lifted them when he got to my window.

It took a second for me to realize that he was waiting for me to lower the glass, and when I did, I raised my hand to the button slowly, my fingers like ice—cold and stiff—as I pushed the button down to allow him access to us. I waited impatiently to see what he was going to do. Would he kill us right then and there? Would he force us to follow him? Arrest us for some made-up crime? My mind raced with the incredible possibilities.

"Thank you for stopping," he said, a strange greeting from an officer if I'd ever heard one. "I mean you no harm."

I furrowed my brow, perplexed by his candor. "What do you want, then?"

"I want to help you, just like I told you before."

"Did you follow us here?"

He offered a quick nod. "I had to wait to talk to you until after you'd left Fallen Oaks."

"What does that mean?" I asked, hearing Cole ask the same question in a whisper behind me. Apparently, the questioning was being left up to me.

"I want to help you kids, but I can't do it inside of Fallen Oaks. It isn't safe."

"What do you mean it isn't safe?" I asked, cocking my head to the side in ignorance, though I suspected we both knew I had some inclination.

In confirmation of my suspicion, he looked over his shoulder, leaning down even closer to me before his answer came. "I think I know what happened to your parents."

"You know who killed them?"

"I think so," he said. "But if I'm right, we could all be in a lot of danger. It's why I had to wait for you to leave, and why I couldn't contact you while you were still there. I needed to catch up with you away from Fallen Oaks."

"But...you're the police. If someone is a threat to you, who in the world is safe?" Cassie asked, popping her head around the seat to ask the question that had haunted me since we'd made our revelation.

He ran a palm across his red forehead. "I wish I knew," he said.

"So, what are you saying?" I asked him.

"I found some evidence in the case files I was digging up from your parents' deaths. Altered files, missing documents. Things that didn't necessarily add up. I wouldn't have thought much of it—I guess, those things happen—but when I was talking to some of the other detectives, I was warned to stay out of the case. They claimed there was nothing to find...which is just about the worst thing you can say to a detective. So, for one detective to say it to another, especially in a case that lacks investigation and makes up for it in missing data and sloppy casework...well, let's just say, something isn't adding up. I've been watching you to see when you'd leave town. I needed to find a chance to catch you."

"But why would you want to help us? You're one of them."

He huffed. "I'm an officer of the law, Miss Delanoe. I graduated at the top of my class and worked my ass—er," he looked at Cassie and quickly corrected his language, though it was futile because she'd heard much worse, "*butt,* off to get where I am. I won't let some half-assed investigation or a couple of bad cops mess up what I've worked for. I do what's right, no matter who it hurts. That's the only reason I became a cop. The only reason I followed in my father's footsteps. To do what's right."

"And what's right in this case, Detective?" I challenged, still not sure we could trust him.

He chuckled. "Damned if I know, kid. I was hoping you'd help me with that."

CHAPTER TWENTY

October 5th
The Anniversary

"Why should we trust you?" I asked the question I knew we all desperately wanted to know. We sat across from Detective McDuffy in a busy coffee shop, just enough noise around us to drown out the conversation.

"What choice do you have?" he asked, the frankness of his words catching me off guard. "Why would I be here if I weren't trying to help you?"

"Because you're planning to kill us?" Gray asked, one copper eyebrow higher than the other as he studied the detective.

"If I wanted to kill you, you'd be dead already," the detective said, chuckling slightly at his own joke, though none of us laughed along. "Look, I'm here because I want to help, plain and simple. I was transferred to Fallen Oaks because I wanted a promotion and there was an opening. I grew up about six hours north of you all, and it always seemed like a nice town. Quiet, ya know? When they gave me your case, it was basically shoved down toward the bottom of my caseload. No one seemed too interested in it. In fact, I remember asking about it when I'd first started, and they said it was a dead end. So, imagine my surprise when a few months later, I received your phone call."

"And what makes you think you can solve the case when everyone else seems to want to bury it? Even if we know the truth, why does it matter when the only people who can enforce the laws are dead set on looking the other way? That's *if* they aren't the ones who should be arrested in the first place." Gray was saying more than I thought he should've. He wanted to believe the detective. He was choosing to trust him when we had no reason to. I wasn't so foolish. He had kind enough eyes, sure, and his story was believable, but he was a cop first and foremost. I couldn't believe he'd willingly betray his job duty to help us. Life had taught me just five years ago to the date that no one was to be trusted.

Still, I sat quietly, letting Gray take the lead for once. He was full of questions while I was full of resentment and silence, unable to piece together my scrambled thoughts.

"I don't know if I can solve the case," the detective said, "but that doesn't mean I don't want to know the truth and help keep you safe." He paused, folding his hands together on the table. "If we can find out the truth, if we can get the answers you guys are looking for—even if it means the murderers will never face the consequences of their actions—would you still want to know?"

Gray looked at me, but I looked down. I couldn't answer that. What would be worse? Knowing the truth but being unable to see justice served? Or forever wondering but never truly knowing? I picked the skin around my thumb, though it was already raw and on the verge of bleeding. I would've given anything to have had my journal in that moment. I needed the solitude…just a few quiet moments to write down my thoughts.

Apparently, Dr. Porter's methods had worked better than I'd realized.

Finally, Gray answered. "I want to know the truth no matter what happens. It would help me move on."

"Me too," Monica agreed quickly.

Cole sat quietly, apparently as lost in his own thoughts as I was. Cassie nodded but never spoke.

"I need to know what you all know," the detective said, his eyes locked on me. I could feel the stares, though I refused to meet his eyes. Apparently he was able to read into my unintentional leadership, despite the fact that Gray was leading the conversation. "Whatever you've found out could help me to piece together the rest of the puzzle."

All too eager to help, Gray began, "We don't know a whole lot, honestly. All we know for sure is what Marg—"

"What do *you* know?" I asked, finally finding my voice. My heart raced, my ears burning red. I looked at the detective with narrowing eyes.

He seemed taken aback by the question. "Pardon me?"

How pretentious are you, dude? "I asked what you know. You have to have found some piece of evidence that made you track us down."

He seemed annoyed by the question but cleared his throat and answered patiently nonetheless. "I told you there were missing files—things that didn't add up about the case."

I shrugged. "Well, we don't know anything. So, if you want to solve the case, it's going to be up to you. We came back to Fallen Oaks to say goodbye to our parents' graves, and now we're going back to our homes to hopefully put this all behind us." I scooted back on the booth's seat. "You asked whether we want to know the truth, detective, and I can't speak for everyone here. But as for me, I'm not interested in the truth anymore. No matter who killed our parents, they're dead. No matter what evidence you find, no matter who deserves to be punished for what happened, they aren't coming back." I shook my head, refusing to let the tears I felt stinging my eyes fall. "Now, I'm going to have to leave. I'm sorry you wasted a trip. If you guys want to come with me, you should come now." For once, I was thankful I'd been the one to drive us. My statement was met by a combination of confused and angered looks.

"What are you talking about?" Gray asked.

"I'm leaving," I said again, standing up from the booth to further prove my point. I reached out, tugging at Cassie's arm. "Who else is coming?"

Slowly, the remainder of the group stood with me. Gray's face showed frustration, but he didn't bother arguing.

"Don't you want to go over what we both know?" Detective McDuffy asked, his voice an octave higher as he watched us preparing to leave. His Adam's apple bobbed as he swallowed.

"No, thank you," I told him with as much politeness as I could muster. I thought he would try to protest further, but to my surprise, he simply nodded.

"Well, suit yourself. Take care, then," he said.

"You too," I called casually, leading the group from the coffee shop quickly. I held my breath until I made it to the car, not checking to see if he was following us. I was sure he would be. Just like I was sure he was lying about everything he'd said.

"What the hell, Ellie?" Gray complained as soon as we'd shut the car doors. He whipped the seatbelt across his chest in anger. "Don't you even care about the truth? Don't you want to know what happened to them?"

"I know what happened to them," I spat in anger. "I was there, remember?"

"We were all there," Cole said. I couldn't tell whose side he was on.

"That was our chance," Gray argued. "To finally know the truth about everything."

"Whose truth?" I challenged. "Because the cops' truth is different than Margaret's. And Margaret's truth is different than Mr. Winters'. And Mr. Winters' truth is different than Mr. Thompson's. And Mr. Thompson's truth is different than ours. And ours is different than our parents'. Don't you get it, Gray? No matter whose side of things we hear, we're never going to know the truth. And talking to that detective was only putting us in more danger."

"So what? We just give up?" he demanded.

"I don't care what any of you do. I'm going home. I have a job. Cassie has school. When I agreed to go to Fallen Oaks, I only promised one day. I said we could turn in the notes and see our parents' graves. We've done that. I've held up my end of the deal. If you guys want to play detective, you can drive yourselves there and do it on your own time."

"Where is all this coming from?" Cole asked. He wasn't angry, as far as I could tell. His voice was filled mostly with concern.

"I don't trust him."

"Who? *Me?*" Gray asked defensively.

"No, not you. Detective McDuffy," I corrected with a scowl. "You all seem to trust him, only God knows why. But I don't. He's still a cop. His loyalty should lie with the rest of his force. And if the Fallen Oaks police department had anything to do with our parents' murders, I can't believe we'd be safe talking to one of their own…or staying anywhere near that town."

"Who can we trust, then?" The question came from my right, the quiet voice of my sister, whose wide eyes met mine with fear.

When I answered, the truth left my lips with an ominous tone that settled into the car quickly. "Honestly, I'm not even sure we can trust each other."

CHAPTER TWENTY-ONE

October 5th

When we arrived back at my apartment, my legs were stiff from driving and my bladder was screaming at me to be emptied. The long car ride had not been kind to any of us. Monica had slept most of the way, her head bouncing against the window whenever we hit a pothole or bump that couldn't be avoided. Beside her, Gray had been awake but absolutely silent for hours. His arms were crossed over his chest in an all-out sulk as he stared out the window. I knew he disagreed with my choice, but it was his decision to follow me. Granted, I was his ride, but that wasn't my fault either.

Regardless, the two people who seemed somewhat on my side—or at least not against me—Cassie and Cole, had spoken a few words here and there on our drive home, giving me enough proof that they didn't hate me, but not entirely enough to know they believed I'd been right in my decision.

As we climbed from the car, I stretched loudly and almost involuntarily, my hands up over my head as a yawn tore from my throat. My passengers made their way toward the trunk, waiting for me to press the button on the fob that would open the compartment and free their luggage. One by one, they gathered their things, leaving my trunk empty except for a pair of jumper cables and an empty Dr. Pepper bottle. I closed it after removing my own bag, and we stared at each other in awkward silence.

I knew we had to be thinking the same thing: what were we supposed to do now? How was it supposed to end? Once again, we were walking away from each other after feeling like we'd gone through life-changing events, with little more to say than 'goodbye.' They weren't my family. They weren't even my friends, if I was being honest. I hadn't spoken to most of them in years and, truth be told, we probably wouldn't speak again for years to come, if ever. Why then was it so hard to say goodbye to them? Harder than it had been to say goodbye to my own flesh-and-blood grandmother.

"I guess I'll see you guys around," Cole filled the silence, shrugging one shoulder casually.

"Yeah, see you," Gray said. The anger that radiated from him earlier had dissipated.

Cole cleared his throat. "You, um, you all…ya know, take care of yourselves." He was staring straight at me as he said it, his bag slung over his shoulder.

I nodded, looking over each of them. This time felt final, and somehow I was sure in my bones I'd never see any of them again. "Take care of yourself, too." I met Gray's eyes then. "All of you."

One by one, the group separated, offering awkward half-smiles and good-byes as they headed toward their cars and Cassie and I headed toward our apartment. So much had changed since we'd seen it last. It was as if I was seeing it through a new set of eyes—eyes now painted with an extra dose of tragedy.

"Do I have to go to school tomorrow?" Cassie asked as I slid the key into the first deadbolt. I nodded, thinking less about her needing to go to school and more about myself needing peace and quiet. *Guardian of the year here, ladies and gentlemen.*

She sighed loudly, apparently finally feeling at ease enough to let her pre-teen show. I wanted to scold her. How dare she be mad about such trivial things after all we'd gone through? But how could I? That's what they don't tell you about surviving a tragedy—real life just keeps going, and you have to deal with it. You don't get a break from the menial errands and annoying things about everyday life just because you've experienced loss. How could I teach her to be grateful for the life that was almost ripped away from her when I complained myself when the sink sprung a leak or the neighbor's dog pooped in the walkway. Life kept on going, and the annoying things stayed annoying.

I pushed open the door but stopped short as I saw what—or who—was waiting for me. My arm went out instinctively to protect Cassie, though my arm would do nothing to stop the bullet. The masked intruder held the gun out, saying nothing as I watched in what felt like slow motion as they pulled the trigger. The bullet sped toward me before I could blink, let alone move, and the icy cold metal tore through my flesh as if it were paper. The pain was white hot; it knocked me backward instantly. As I began to fall, I noticed the curtain blowing in the breeze from the window they'd broken to come inside. My first thought as the blood began to pool from the wound on my collarbone was not about Cassie, though she was definitely my second thought, or about my parents, or even about the fact that I didn't feel ready to die. It was about the window being broken. The fact that leaves had blown into my once-meticulous apartment. Who would be left to clean it up? What would they think about the mess I'd left? About the kind of person who'd leave a mess like that? I guess fear can do that to you. Jumble up your thoughts until they make no logical sense.

The masked intruder moved toward us, toward Cassie, and I whimpered, wanting to beg her to run. I sank to the ground, barely aware of Cassie's screams as my body dropped, and she tried to hold my weight though we both knew her attempts were futile. Her fear-filled face was just inches from mine, and as her tears leaked onto my face, one more thought crossed my mind before I faded into the darkness with a crack of my skull to the concrete: *I was right,* I thought, *I'll never see any of them again.*

CHAPTER TWENTY-TWO

October 6th

When I opened my eyes, I was in heaven. Bright, white lights shone down on me from above as thick clouds blurred my vision. An angel spoke my name just to my right, and I turned toward the muddled voice, unable to make out their face. I smiled, only half-aware of anything that was happening. Where had I been? Where was I going?

As my vision began to find focus, I blinked heavily, staring in awe as the clouds disappeared from my eyes. Wherever I was, I was beginning to doubt it was heaven.

"Can you hear me? Are you with us?" a stern voice asked to my left. I turned my head slightly, staring at the figure dressed in a white coat. *Doctor.* The word came to me slightly delayed, but it was there. "Ellie, are you with me?" he asked again.

To my right, a hand slid into mine, gripping it with force. I looked toward the person without answering the doctor. It should've been Cassie, but I knew it wasn't. Instead, gray eyes met mine. I took in his ashen expression. He looked away from me quickly, staring at the doctor.

"Why isn't she answering?" he demanded.

I looked back at the doctor. Why wasn't I? Why couldn't I form the words that my mind knew? I tried to shake my head, but it was as if my muscles had forgotten how. Had I hit my head? What happened? I couldn't remember.

The doctor sighed, resting a hand on my arm while Cole held the other. Where was Cassie? "We'll know more once we get all of the test results back. It's very likely that she just needs a bit more time to recover."

"Here," I said, surprising myself as the word escaped my throat. Both men looked at me in shock.

"Ellie?" Cole was up out of his chair in an instant. "Can you hear me?"

"Yes," I croaked. Again, I was shocked that I could remember how to make my mouth work. Just seconds ago, it had felt impossible.

He nodded his head at the doctor, his mouth hanging open in what seemed like relief as he looked back at me.

"Do you remember what happened?" Cole asked, his voice breathy.

The doctor took hold of my temple before I could answer and gently turned my head toward him. He lifted a narrow flashlight from his breast pocket and shone it in my eye, blinking it once and then switching it to the next eye. "I'm Dr. Owl, like the bird." He smiled warmly, his walnut skin creasing around his eyes. "How do you feel?" the doctor asked, overruling Cole's question.

"Sore," I said stiffly, trying to adjust in vain. My answer was correct—I was incredibly sore. In short bursts, my memories came back to me. I remembered the intruder in my apartment. I remembered the gunshot. I looked down to my shoulder, waiting to see the wound, but my gown and what looked like an oversized bandage blocked my view. My body was the pure definition of juxtaposition in and of itself. I was in pain while also feeling numb, exhausted while also feeling like I'd been sleeping for years. There were a million questions on my mind: what had happened to me? Was I going to be okay? Had my assailant been caught? But the most important question needed to be answered first. "Where's Cassie?" I asked.

Cole cleared his throat, and I felt his grip tighten on my hand. "She's fine. She's in the cafeteria. Gone to get a drink." He smirked. "First time she's left your side since last night."

"Last night?" I demanded, shocked by his words. "How long have I been out?"

"You lost a lot of blood," the doctor answered. "Do you remember what happened?"

"I was…I was shot," I said, the words more of a question than a true answer. I waited for him to nod, urging me to go on before I did. "I don't remember much else."

"Did you get a good look at the person?" Cole asked, directing my attention back toward him.

Before I could answer, the doctor cut him off. "The police will want to ask her those questions. I'll have a nurse page the detectives to let them know she's awake." He raised a brow to Cole. "Could you stay with her?"

"Of course," Cole vowed, sounding like he was taking his responsibilities way too seriously to be what they were. I was bedridden and sore; there was no chance I'd be a trouble to keep an eye on.

"I'll be right back," the doctor told me, his words resonating like a warning to me. His onyx eyes held mine for a moment too long before he turned, his coat flapping behind him like a cape as he disappeared through the wooden door. Once he was gone, I narrowed my sights back on Cole.

"How did you find out about me? Why are you here?"

He colored fiercely, and a muscled tensed along his jaw. "I heard the gunshot before I'd made it to my car. I don't know how, but I knew it was you. I ran back as quickly as I could. By the time I got to you, the attacker was gone and Cassie was in hysterics. I called the police, but Detective McDuffy was already there. Apparently, he doesn't take 'no' for an answer very well."

"The detective was at my apartment?"

He nodded, his lips puckering with slight annoyance. "I guess he followed us. Don't be too mad, though. The doctors say he may have saved your life. He was the only one with enough resolve to stay calm, and he knew a bit about basic medical care. He had a towel wrapped around your shoulder and he was—" Suddenly, his voice broke, and I watched as his mouth opened in dismay. "I thought you were going to die. We all did."

A tumble of confused thoughts and conflicting emotions assailed me. "W-wh..." I paused, trying to piece together the words that had fragmented in my mind. "I didn't know you cared so much."

He hesitated, measuring me for a moment before conceding. "I didn't either. Honestly, the ride to the hospital and these past few hours, waiting to see when—*if*—you'd wake up, it was miserable."

I swallowed hard, trying to manage some feeble answer while my head swam with uncertainty. "Well, I'm awake now," I whispered, clearing my throat in an attempt to erase the awkwardness of our tension. "Did you call Monica and Gray?"

"They're going to try to make it. They were both almost home before I thought to call them." His fingers laced through mine, causing my stomach to twist into knots. "I'm just so glad you're okay."

I smiled, hoping I was giving off an air of effortlessness that I certainly wasn't feeling. "Thank you," I said. "And I don't blame them if they can't make it. We all needed to get back to our normal lives as soon as possible, anyway." I took a deep breath, trying to relax when a thought filled my head. "Is the detective still here?"

He cocked his head to one side, and I could sense his agitation. Apparently, the tension over the detective's imposition into our lives hadn't changed, despite him saving my life. "No, he left earlier. I'm sure he'll be back, though. He's been popping in now and again to check on you."

"You didn't see the person?" I asked, trying desperately to recall the memory from my mind.

Again, he shook his head. "I'm sorry. I wish I had. They must've gone the opposite way. By the time I got back to you, it was just you, Cassie, and McDuffy alone. She told me they were wearing a mask, but she didn't get too good a look at them either. Cassie said McDuffy was the only reason the intruder didn't shoot her. He yelled 'police' after he heard the first shot, and the guy took off out the side door." Cold chills ran up and down my arm as his thumb stroked my knuckles, and he scooted closer toward me. "We're going to find out who it was," he promised, his slate eyes burning into mine with a fire that assured me he was telling the truth. "I promise you we will. Nothing like this will—"

"Don't say that." I shied away, pulling my hand from his grasp. "Don't make promises you can't keep."

"Who says I can't keep—"

"We still have no idea who killed our parents," I told him. "Or who left us the letters. So, even if they're all the same person...why would we be able to catch them now? I just...I can't..." I sucked in a deep breath, trying to calm my nerves before I spoke. "I can't be fooled with false hope right now, okay?"

He looked down. When he lifted his eyes back to meet mine, the pain still lingered there. His words, though, gave no evidence of emotion. "Okay. I understand." He scooted his chair back just a few inches as the door opened again and the doctor returned with Cassie by his side.

As she saw me, a cry of relief bubbled from her lips and she rushed toward me, her fair hair brushed into disarray by her quick movements. "Ellie," she sobbed, pressing her face into my uninjured shoulder. "Oh my God..." Words escaped her mouth, coming out in quick, unintelligible bursts, and I felt her hot tears soaking through my gown. I leaned my head onto hers, unable to move my wounded arm enough to comfort her like I wanted.

"Shh," I whispered, feeling cool tears fill my own eyes as I realized just how frightened she'd been. What would she have done without me? How would she have fared losing yet another relative at such a young age. Fight as we did, she still needed me. "It's okay. I'm okay."

She pulled back, brushing the wispy hair from her face and wiping her tears. "Are you?" she asked. "Is she going to be okay?" She turned to face the doctor then, one hand still firmly on my arm.

The doctor nodded patiently, glancing at the iPad in his

hands before answering. "She's going to be just fine eventually. You were lucky the detective was there to minimize your blood loss, but all in all, your injuries were repairable. Your humerus and clavicle were both shattered by the bullet," as he spoke, he moved a long finger across his shoulder to show the bones he was talking about, "but we were able to repair them. On the surface, you'll be healed in about three months, but the bones will likely take longer. Based on the extent of your injuries, but taking into account that you are young and in good health, I'd say you're looking at closer to six months to be completely back to normal. You'll wear a sling for at least three, and you'll need to start physical therapy to strengthen the torn muscles."

"Six *months?*" I practically shouted at him. I had no medical knowledge to speak of, so I was thinking it would be more like six weeks at most. "Will I still be able to work?"

"Depending on your job, as long as you aren't required to use that arm, I don't see any reason why you shouldn't be able to. If it starts disrupting your healing, you might need to cut back. But, for now, let's just focus on resting, okay?"

"When do I get to go home?" I asked, sensing that he was about to disappear from the room again. I was aching to get out of that bed. "My sister has school."

"We're going to take it one day at a time," he said, his tone light but firm. "Ten to fourteen days, most likely, barring any complications. We're going to be watching for signs of infection for a few days, at least. As long as everything remains satisfactory, we'll get you out of here as quickly as we can. As for your sister's school, it's likely you'll need to find a relative who can get her there for a while, because there's no chance you'll be out sooner than a week."

"I don't have any family who can help with that. There's

no way I can miss a week of work or keep her out of school for a week. You have to let me out sooner."

His left eyebrow raised a fraction. "Do you have someone who can help you with transitioning home after we release you? Because if not, we may not be able to release you on time, let alone sooner. You may need to be admitted to a rehab program in order to build up your arm strength. Atrophy is a very real risk in injuries like this."

"I'll be fine," I assured him, my heart racing as I considered all the factors: the mountain of medical debt that was sure to bankrupt me, the fact that my sister would soon be labeled as truant and me thrown in jail if I didn't have her back to school soon, and the fact that my only living relative was a grandmother who wanted little to do with us and certainly wouldn't be traipsing across the country to help us.

The doctor laughed under his breath, further infuriating me as he did so. "I'm sure you will, Ellie, but the fact remains—"

"I can stay with her." The voice came from my right, and I looked over at Cole in horror.

"No, you can't!" I said quickly, not bothering to entertain the offer at all. "I'll be fine. Honestly, I will. I can call Cassie's school and let them know what's happened. Surely they'll understand something like this."

Cole pursed his lips, looking up at the doctor and disregarding what I'd said. "Can she go home without someone there to help her?"

"Ideally, no," the doctor said, shaking his head. "And, if that's the *only* option, it may delay her release."

It felt as though they were teaming up against me, and I really didn't like it. I huffed. It wasn't like I hated the idea of Cole helping me, but it would be awkward. He wouldn't fit into the routine I so desperately wanted to slip back into. And what would Cassie think? Besides that, I hardly knew Cole. None of what we'd gone through had changed that.

My hand was still clasped in his, and I looked over at him, trying to go over my options in my still-drowsy mind. As a yawn escaped, betraying the exhaustion I was trying to contain, Cole smiled at me. "We can discuss this later. You should get some rest. Don't worry. I'll be right here with Cassie when you wake up again."

I shook my head, prepared to argue, but couldn't speak as another yawn tore its way from my mouth involuntarily. Finally, I nodded, closing my eyes as sleep began to find me again. Before I could fall peacefully to sleep, I heard the door open again, and my eyes shot open. Cassie stepped back from my bed, letting men in suits walk into the room. Neither of them were Detective McDuffy, but from their professional demeanor and attire, I put together that they must be law enforcement.

Instead of allowing me to remain in suspense for too long, one of the men spoke up. "Hello, Ellie. I'm Detective Glascow. This is my partner, Detective Sullivan." He pulled out a notepad from his jacket pocket, clicking the pen so that the ballpoint protruded. "We need to ask you a few questions about what happened to you."

I nodded, though my stomach tightened as I did. My memory of the event was fuzzy at best. What could I possibly tell them? And what if I got it wrong?

"There's no need to be nervous," Sullivan said, reading my expression without a word from me. "If you don't remember or don't know the answer, just tell us that. We only want to help catch the person who did this."

Again, I nodded, running the white sheet at my waist between my fingers nervously. "Okay."

Detective Glascow spoke first. "First of all, can you tell us what you remember about what happened?"

I closed my eyes for a moment, wanting to recall what happened while also terrified about reliving it. "I…I walked into my apartment with Cassie."

"Was the door locked?" Sullivan asked.

"Yes, er, I think." I paused, chewing on my lip. Had it been? I put my key in, right? I sighed. "I don't remember. I think so." I looked at Cassie, who wasn't responding. She looked down at the floor.

"Cassie's been asked not to answer during your interview," Detective Glascow answered the question I hadn't asked. "She's already given us her version of events."

"I…don't understand."

"We just want to get a clear picture of what happened. It's normal for some of the events of the night to get a bit blurred, but we don't want your version to muddle what Cassie remembers, and vice versa. It's our job to put it all together once we hear from both of you," he said.

"Okay, I don't remember if the door was locked. I thought I put the key in the lock…" I trailed off. "But if it was unlocked, me unlocking it wouldn't have mattered."

The detective wrote something down in his notepad before clearing his throat. "Okay. Go on…you opened the door. Then what?"

"He was there. The man."

"You know it was a man?" Sullivan asked.

"I, um, well…no. I guess I don't know for sure. They were dressed in black with a mask on. Their clothes were baggy. I couldn't be sure that it was a man, but that was my first guess."

"What happened when you saw them? Did it seem like you were interrupting a robbery? Did they have anything in their hands?"

"Just…the gun," I said, my eyes focusing on the wall as they filled with tears, the picture forming so clearly in my mind, it was as if it was happening again. "It was like he, she, whoever…it was like they were waiting for us. Maybe they just heard us coming, I don't know, but they were standing just a few feet from the door. The gun raised as soon as they saw us. There wasn't time to move or think. I…I remember the noise, the way it cracked through the air. And I remember falling. I remember worrying about Cassie," I looked at her, "but that's it."

"Does anyone have access to your apartment? Anyone you've given a key to?"

"No," I answered quickly. "I don't trust anyone. The only person with a key aside from Cassie and me would be someone who works for my apartment complex."

"Anyone you can think of who'd want to hurt you?"

I nodded instantly. "I was one of the Fallen Oaks Five." I watched to see if recognition filled the detectives' faces, but I couldn't be certain. "Five years ago, a group of people killed everyone in my subdivision except me, him, her," I pointed to Cole and Cassie, "and two others. We recently got letters that we believe came from those killers warning us that they'd be coming back to finish the job."

Sullivan raised a brow. "Okay. What did you do with the letters? Did you call the police?"

"We turned the letters over to the Fallen Oaks Police Department."

The detectives nodded in unison as Detective Glascow tucked the notebook back into his pocket. "Thank you, Ellie."

"So, what now? What will happen?"

"We've got our team going over forensics at the scene. Checking for fingerprints, points of access, and DNA. If we find anything, we'll go from there. We'll be in touch with what we learn," Detective Sullivan said, his eyes darting toward Cassie. There was something they weren't saying, but what was it? What wouldn't they tell me, and why?

"What about my apartment? Can I go back to it?" Did I even want to? I swallowed, trying not to let the fear show.

Detective Glascow looked at my doctor. "Your doctor says you'll be here for a few more days. Our team will be done at your apartment by then, and it'll be turned back over to you. For now, it's being treated as a crime scene, and we're allowing no access."

"Okay," I said. What else could I say? I knew the drill all too well. It wasn't my first time living in a crime scene.

CHAPTER TWENTY-THREE

October 9th

"Where's your friend?" a pretty, young nurse asked as she walked into my hospital room. She glanced at one of the monitors, typing something into her iPad before glancing back up to me.

"He took my sister to school," I told her. "He'll be back soon."

"He's cute, isn't he?" she asked with a smirk.

"He is," I said. It was true. Cole *was* cute. Even in his anger-filled, badly aging state, he was still a guy who could make you do a double take. That had never changed.

"You two aren't together, are you?" she asked. "Is he single?"

I felt a pang of worry filling my stomach. He was single, as far as I knew, but how could anyone deal with the baggage he carried. Feeling instantly guilty for having thought that, I nodded. "He is."

"Cool," she said. "Can I get you anything? Breakfast will

be up soon," she said, placing the iPad between her arm and her waist.

"I'm fine, thank you, though."

She smiled, turning to walk out of the room. "Let me know if you need anything. Just buzz, okay?"

I nodded, watching her leave. I wasn't sure why I felt so jealous. It wasn't like I cared about Cole in that way. I was sure I didn't, but somehow I felt protective of him. That wasn't my place either, but there it was. The idea of an outsider dating him caused my anxiety to take root. I forced the thought from my head. *Not my circus, not my monkeys.*

Cole was a grown man, and he could do whatever he chose. As if conjured by thought, the door to my room opened again and Cole appeared. He smirked at me as he strolled into the room. "Safe and sound in class," he told me, already anticipating my first question.

"And you explained to the principal what's going on?"

"I told him exactly what you told me to tell him." He sank down in the chair next to me and grabbed the remote. "Any preferences?"

"What did he say, Cole?"

He looked back at me. "He understood. Everything's fine. Cassie's fine. You're fine. I'm fine. Just...relax." His tone was surprisingly calming as he flipped through the channels, finally deciding on a sitcom I couldn't help but roll my eyes at.

"How's your hand?" I asked as I watched him picking mindlessly at the edge of the gauze bandage one of the nurses had placed over his wound.

"Better," he assured me. "Have the nurses been in to check on you?"

"Mhm," I said. "Hey, how do you think Cassie's dealing

with all of this? I mean, really. Do you think she's okay? Maybe calling my grandma to keep her for a while might be the best thing."

"Do you really believe that?" he challenged. "It seems to me like Cassie is happiest wherever you are. She needs you almost as much as you need her."

I pursed my lips. "I don't think that's true."

"I know it is," he said, his eyes locking with mine. He held my gaze for a few seconds too long, and I broke eye contact awkwardly.

"So, um, that nurse…I think she likes you."

He rolled his eyes playfully. "Which one?"

"The short one with red hair. She asked if you were single."

"She's cute," he said with a shrug, turning back toward the TV.

"Are you going to ask her out?" I pushed the conversation forward.

"Nah," he said, not elaborating any further.

"Why not?" I asked. "You don't like her?"

"You and I both know I have way too many issues to try to start a new relationship. Been there, done that…trust me, it's never pretty." He paused. "What about you? Why aren't you dating anyone?"

"Who says I'm not?"

"Uh, probably the fact that we've been gone all this time and you haven't once mentioned or called any sort of significant other."

I snorted. "Fair enough. Yeah, like you said…issues."

"Well, if nothing else, I guess we've got a bright future in movie franchises. Fallen Oaks Five, I mean, if that's not a superhero group, I don't know what is."

I furrowed my brow at him. Was he trying to make a joke? "Did you really just say that?"

He snorted. "Oh, come on, you have to admit it was funny."

"What would your superpower be?"

"Superhuman fists, of course." He gestured toward his bandaged hand. "And yours?"

"Protection," I said without having to think. "I'd want to be able to shield my family from evil."

He swallowed, the conversation taken from fun to dark in an instant. It wasn't intentional, but once the sentence had left my mouth, there was nothing I could do. Finally, he said, "Okay, so you're defense, and I'm offense. Sounds like we'd make an excellent team."

"Yeah," I admitted, "I think it's fair to say we would."

"What about everyone else?" he asked. "What would the rest of the group have for a superpower?" He thought for a moment. "Gray's easy, right? Fire, because of the hair," he gestured toward his own hair as if to explain an already obvious point.

"Monica would be able to hear thoughts. She's so quiet, that would be perfect for her."

His head bobbed in agreement. "And Cassie…"

"Cassie's superpower would be to heal. She's so motherly and kind. That's the perfect power for her."

He smiled at me, his expression warm, and cleared his throat. "Well, I guess she's exactly what we need, then." He winked, holding his sore fist out to me. I bumped it gently as his voice grew low and he said, "Fallen Oaks Five to the rescue. It's a movie deal waiting to happen."

Pain crept into my sleep, pulling me from it quickly. I opened my eyes, staring around the hospital room. I could see the darkness of the night creeping in from behind the curtains, despite the brightness of my room.

Cole was asleep in an uncomfortable position in one of the chairs they'd brought in for him, while Cassie was sleeping in the spare hospital bed designed for my roommate, though I had none.

I reached for the call button, wincing in pain. My whole body ached, and though I tried to be quiet, reaching behind me to grab the button sent a shockwave through my body and caused me to whimper involuntarily. Cole's eyes were open in an instant, and he was at my side. The man was practically a robot. I couldn't see how he'd gotten more than a few hours sleep in the week since I'd been in the hospital, and yet he'd never once been grouchy or short with me and was always ready at a moment's notice to help me.

As much as I hated to admit it, I really wasn't sure what I would've done without him there to help me. Cassie had been great, but I could only put so much on her. I wanted her to focus on school and returning to her normal life. I didn't want her to see my pain any more than she had to.

"What is it? What's wrong?"

"I'm...just a little sore. Can you push the button?"

He nodded, reaching over my head and pushing it instantly. "Done. What can I get for you? Are you thirsty? Need another blanket?"

I was shivering, but I was pretty sure it was only from the adrenaline of the night. "I'm fine," I told him. "Promise."

"How badly are you hurting?" he asked.

"Pretty badly," I admitted. "Did they skip my medicine, you

think?" I looked up at the whiteboard on the wall that listed my medicine along with the times I'd taken it. It had been six hours since my last dose, while I was used to taking it every four.

Cole noticed the error as quickly as I did. "I'll go see what's taking so long," he said, not waiting for a response as he disappeared out of the room. A few moments later, he returned with a nurse in tow.

"You're starting to feel a little pain?" the nurse asked, checking one of the monitors.

"Yeah," I said.

"It's been two extra hours since her last dose. They've only been waiting four, but she's gone six," Cole said. "What's going on?"

"Well, it could've just been done and not logged on the board, so let me check her chart," the nurse retorted. "Hmm, nope. It looks like they skipped your last dose because you were asleep. Do you want to go ahead and take it now or wait a few more hours and keep on schedule?" I didn't think it was possible for me to wait another minute, let alone two more hours.

"Now, please," I squeaked out.

"Alright," she said casually, as if I'd suggested she get her nails done rather than bring me medication. "Let me go see about getting that for you." She pressed a button on her iPad before turning to leave the room. As the door shut, I heard Cole click his tongue.

"You hanging in there?" he asked.

I nodded, biting my tongue to keep the tears at bay. I didn't want him to know how badly I was hurting because I didn't want him to see me as weak. I was just a few hours overdue for some medication, and I felt as though someone had ripped a brand new bullet hole through my body. I was being ridiculous.

He studied my face for a moment, one hand on the edge of my bed. "It's really bad, isn't it?"

I tried not to think of it by changing the subject to a sleeping Cassie. I nodded my head in her direction. "She must really be tired to sleep through all of this."

"Ellie," he said with a stern tone.

"What?" I asked.

He frowned. "You don't have to be brave right now. Is it bad?"

Feeling the wall in me collapse and flood my eyes with fresh tears, I nodded. "Yes," I squeaked.

He darted from the room without another word, returning moments later with my doctor. "She's in pain. She needs something *now,*" he told Dr. Owl, huffing out a breath from his apparent jog down the hall.

The doctor looked between us with wide eyes. "I'm very sorry, Ellie. Let me take a look at your chart." He pulled it up on the iPad in his hands and nodded. "Ahh, yes. I can see why you'd be in pain. You missed your last dose. Let's get that fixed right now, shall we?"

I nodded as I heard Cole's voice, still full of anger. "This can't happen again," he told him. "She should've never been allowed to sleep through her dose. You people wake her up all the time for every reason under the sun, but you didn't wake her for this? How could you be so careless?"

"We'll make sure it doesn't happen again," Doctor Owl said, and I felt him touching my mouth to open it. "Let's get a temp while I'm here, Ellie." I lifted my tongue, allowing him to insert the thermometer.

"You're going to be okay now," Cole told me, and I hoped it was true.

"It's a good thing you have someone who cares for you so deeply in your corner," Doctor Owl said as the thermometer beeped and he checked the temp.

"I'm not going anywhere," Cole vowed, watching the doctor closely as he entered the temp into the iPad. "Is she running a fever?"

The doctor smiled dotingly at him. "Not at all. A very good sign. Ellie is proving herself to be a fighter." He paused, looking down at me. A second later, the door opened again, and the nurse was back with a small, clear cup of pills and a freshly refilled glass of water. "Here we go, Ellie," she said, more polite now that the doctor was in the room. "Open up."

I took the pills as if they were my lifeline, closing my eyes as I waited for the relief to kick in. "You should start feeling some relief any moment now."

I nodded. When I opened my eyes, three worried sets of eyes were on me. "I feel better already," I told them, willing it to be true.

"Excellent. I'll be back in a little while to check on you," Doctor Owl said. "Seems like I'm leaving you in good hands."

As if to further prove the point, Cole reached for my hand, taking it gently between the two of his. He watched them leave the room before looking at me. "You're okay now? You swear?"

"I'm better," I told him. "Much."

"I'll set an alarm on my phone so this doesn't happen again. If they aren't in here every four hours, I'll track them down and bring 'em back to you."

"Thank you," I said. "I'm really okay. You should get some rest now."

"I'll stay up a little longer," he told me. His eyes drifted to Cassie, who was still asleep, and I watched him move around the end of my bed and toward her. He moved the cover that had fallen off her body up over her shoulders gently, so that she only stirred just a bit. "She was tired. Long day, I guess," he said.

"You will make an excellent dad someday, Cole," I told him, unable to contain my smile.

"You sound shocked," he said.

"Not shocked necessarily, but I've never seen this side of you," I admitted. "You were always…well, not like this."

"I've never had a chance to be like this," he said. "Teenage boys aren't exactly encouraged to be caring and nurturing. And since their deaths, I haven't been around anyone long enough to care."

"Do you want kids one day?" I asked, the pain medicine kicking in full force as the last drop of pain melted away.

"One day, I hope, but like we said…too many issues. It won't ever happen for me like I want it to."

My jaw dropped. "You don't know that."

He shook off my response. "What about you, Ellie? You're obviously great with Cassie, but do you want a family of your own someday?"

"Cassie is all the family I need," I told him. I'd never done more than briefly consider anything else. I didn't need a family of my own, didn't need to pass on my own problems to an innocent newborn. But Cassie loved me through everything that was horribly wrong with me, and I loved her more than life itself. Wasn't that what a mother did? As far as I was concerned, Cassie was the only child I'd ever need. She'd made me vulnerable enough without needing to add a husband or child to the mix.

"She loves you, but someday she'll do something with her own life. Where does that leave you?" His tone was soft, unaware of the blow he'd just driven straight into my chest. Did he think I didn't already worry about that every single day? Did he think I didn't know that I was a shell of a person without my Cassie-sized crutch? But I wasn't ready to think about what would happen to me when she realized she didn't need me as much as I needed her. My heart just couldn't go there yet.

"All alone, I guess," I said, my voice cracking despite my attempts to maintain my resolve.

"Oh, Ellie." Realizing what he'd done, he was back at my side in an instant. "I'm sorry. I don't even know why I asked that. Cassie loves you. She's not ever going to leave you all alone. It's the middle of the night and I have verbal-diarrhea apparently. Just…ignore me."

I nodded, leaning my head back onto my pillow as the tears began to spill. I couldn't tell him that I wanted her to leave me, no matter how badly it hurt, because I needed to know that I'd done enough, been enough, given enough to make her into a normal human. Wasn't that the curse of being a parent, even a makeshift one, wanting so desperately to keep them yours forever while also hoping you'd given them the confidence to fly the nest and tear your heart out as they went? "I think I'm going to go to sleep," I said finally.

"Of course." I could feel his stare burning into me, but I couldn't look his way. I was too hurt and exhausted to move. "I'm sorry, Ellie," he whispered, his voice lulling me back into the darkness as sleep found me once again.

CHAPTER TWENTY-FOUR

October 12th

"You can change this if you want to. Cole won't mind." I tossed the remote to Cassie, who was planted firmly at the end of my bed, legs tucked up under her.

"It's okay," she said. "It's actually pretty funny."

"This coming from the kid who would only ever watch *Forensic Files* and *SVU*?" I raised a skeptical brow.

She chuckled. "I'm diversifying, okay?"

"Whatever you say," I agreed with a laugh. It was the first chance I'd gotten to talk to her alone since everything had happened and, though I wanted to keep things light, I knew I needed to talk to her about the shooting. "Hey, Cass, how are you doing with, er, everything?"

"I'm fine." She popped a crinkle cut fry into her mouth. "You're the one who got shot, Ellie. You're the one who should be getting checked on."

"That doesn't mean it wasn't terrifying for you, too. You

had to witness everything. Don't discount the trauma that can cause. You of all people should know that."

She trailed the next fry around in the styrofoam tray her lunch had come in, her expression suddenly very serious. "It was really scary, Ellie. I thought I was going to lose you, too." When she looked up at me, fat tears filled her eyes.

I nodded. "I'm sorry you had to go through that."

She sniffled. "I feel stupid, getting upset. It was you who went through the trauma. But thinking about losing you terrifies me. You're all that I have left."

"Hey," I said, trying to calm her down as I saw more tears falling. "I'm right here, okay?" I reached for her arm, but she didn't move toward me. "I'm not going anywhere, and you aren't going to lose me." It was a promise I couldn't guarantee I'd keep, but it was what she needed to hear in that moment.

"You can't," she said, wiping her tears away as quickly as they fell. "When we walked through that door, I didn't see him at first. And then, when I did, it took me a minute to realize what was happening. By that time, it was too late. I remember watching the bullet hit you. It was so fast, Ellie. So fast. You think you know how things like that happen, you know, you see them on TV and stuff, but it's so different in person. I wasn't even sure it was real. And then you were falling and I tried so hard to keep you from hitting the ground, but I was shaking and crying and I couldn't hold you up. He took a step toward us, and I knew he was going to shoot me next and I was terrified, but I couldn't stop crying because I thought you were dead. When I heard Detective McDuffy's voice and the man turned and took off, I don't think I even felt relief. I wasn't scared for myself anymore, sure, but...I really thought I'd lost you." Sobs accompanied her words, her cheeks now coated with salty tears. "I don't know what I'd do if I lost you," she repeated.

"You didn't lose me," I promised her. This time, when I held my arm out to her, she crawled up toward the head of the bed and sank into my chest, mindful of my wounded shoulder. "And you aren't going to, okay? I'm sorry you keep having to go through this stuff."

"I'm sorry, too," she said. "You don't deserve any of it either, and you were just a kid when you got stuck with me. You can't even have your own life because everything has to be about me. It's not fair, Ellie, and I'm so sorry."

"What are you talking about?" I asked her, tucking my chin into my chest so I could look at her better. "*Stuck* with you? Cassie, you're the best thing that ever happened to me. Don't you know that? If anything, you saved my life. You give me a reason to keep fighting when all I really want to do some days is give up. I don't want my own life if it doesn't have you right here." I pulled her in closer toward me. "You need to know that. You've never been and will never be a burden to me. I would do everything all over again, including getting shot, which *hurt,* just to make sure that you're safe."

She sniffled. "I just want you to know that you can have your own life, you know? Like...I can take care of myself."

"I do know that," I said, rubbing my cheek on the top of her head. "But that doesn't mean you should have to. Besides that, I don't know if *I* can take care of *myself.* I still need you, kiddo. Face it, you're stuck with me for a few more years." Tears blurred my vision as I kissed her scalp.

"I think I can handle that,'" she said. She sat up away from me, facing me with a giant smile.

"Oh, you think you can, huh?" I asked with a laugh. "You'd better say that."

She giggled loudly as the door opened and Cole appeared. His eyebrows raised as he saw our tears. "Everything okay?"

"Everything's great," I assured him, watching as he took the seat next to the bed. For the first time in so long, I felt like that could actually be the case.

CHAPTER TWENTY-FIVE

October 18th

Twelve days into my stay at the hospital, the news I'd anxiously waited on finally arrived.

"You're ready to go home," Doctor Owl told me, his smile wide.

I'd been standing up, making my way carefully back from the bathroom when he spoke the words, and I nearly lost my balance. Cole grabbed under my arm to keep me from collapsing completely with excitement.

"Really?" I asked as he steadied me.

The doctor's eyes were warm, as always, as he nodded. "You're healing well, and there've been no complications. I feel comfortable releasing you as long as you feel ready." He looked at Cole. "And as long as she'll have support at home through the coming weeks. Someone to make sure she gets to physical therapy and subsequent appointments."

Cole was nodding before the sentence came to an end as

he helped me toward the bed. "Of course. I'll be there as long as I need to be."

I smiled at him, my insides jittery with excitement. It had been twelve days since I'd stepped foot outside. While the idea of returning to my apartment still caused me anxiety, I longed to be within walls that were my own again. I wanted to go home.

"Very well," the doctor said. "If that's all set, I'll start preparing the release paperwork. It'll be this evening before we let you go, so just sit tight and order your lunch if you haven't already." He pointed toward the cafeteria menu that lay on the tray beside my bed. "I'll be back soon."

"Thank you," I called after him as he exited the room. I looked over to Cole, who was still right at my side as he eased me onto the bed. His excitement visibly matched mine as I squealed.

He laughed. "'Bout time you busted out of here, huh?"

I nodded. "Thank you for staying with me, Cole." It was the first time I'd said it, though he'd stayed with Cassie and I every day since the attack, only leaving my side to take Cassie to and from school every day. "You didn't have to, and I wouldn't have blamed you if you didn't, but it's really meant so much."

He smiled, and I could see that he took the words to heart. "I'm glad I could help. It's the least I could do."

That wasn't true, though, and we both knew it. We weren't friends. Despite growing up in the same subdivision and attending the same school, the only thing that had ever connected us was the loss of our parents. Since that, we'd sent a few occasional texts and kept in touch on the anniversaries, but that was it. We weren't friends. So why had he stayed? He'd never shown any interest in me romantically.

Besides, he was so incredibly out of my league it was ridiculous, so what? What then? What now?

As he set me on the bed and backed away, I smirked at him, trying to make light of what I was about to say. "You know you don't have to stay with me after you get me home. They'll never know the difference, and you've already done more than enough."

He stared at me with concern. "Is that your way of saying you don't want me to stay?"

I shook my head. "No, I just…I mean, I'm sure you need to get back to work."

He scoffed. "I have vacation time."

"Shouldn't you use that for…vacation?"

"You worry too much, Ellie. It's fine, trust me. Your doctor said you need someone to stay with you until you get better. Who else do you have?"

I swallowed, embarrassed to admit the truth we both knew. "No one besides Cassie."

He nodded, looking down at the floor. When he looked back up, his expression had softened considerably. "If I were in your shoes, I'd have even less than that." His half-smile broke my heart as I finally saw the real reason he was there. He was just as lonely as we all were. Somehow, we needed each other. Somehow, once strangers, now we were all each other had.

CHAPTER TWENTY-SIX

October 18th

"Home sweet home," I said sarcastically as we entered the apartment. The blood had been cleaned away, but the stain on the concrete outside of our door remained. I wondered if that would be taken out of my deposit.

I looked around the room, surprised that it looked mostly the same. I don't know what I'd been expecting, but I knew it should've felt different somehow. Except for the stray piece of yellow police tape that had been left behind and the bloodstains I'd seen in the breezeway, I almost wondered if it had been a dream.

Cassie shut the door behind us, scooping up the piece of yellow tape and tossing it into the garbage as if she didn't want me to see it. They wanted to protect me from it all, that much was obvious. Like I'd wanted to protect Cassie all her life. But it was useless. I wasn't likely to forget what happened. It wasn't like the aftermath was even close to over.

As if to prove my point, Cole leaned down and moved the

coffee table out of my way, gesturing for me to sit on the couch. I slid off the shoes the hospital had provided and shook my head. "I want to take a shower. A real shower, in my own apartment."

They knew better than to argue, though I could see them both worrying about the doctor's warning not to get my wound wet. "I'll be fine," I assured them. "Doctor Owl said to make sure to keep the waterproof bandage on there, and it'll be fine."

"Do you need help?" Cassie asked.

"No," I said. Truth was, I wanted to be alone. For the first time in weeks, I wanted a moment alone to process what had happened in the very place I stood. I looked down at the white tile, wondering if the black scuff under my feet had always been there or if the shooter had left it. Would the rest of my time there be spent wondering things like that? Seeing things that I'd never noticed before and wondering if they'd been left by the person who tried to murder me? I shuffled past them without another word, a sudden sob caught in my throat as I made my way down the hallway and toward the bathroom. I heard their quiet voices behind me—they'd become quite the little team since I'd gotten hurt. I couldn't deny that it had me feeling left out, as if they'd formed a club and I was the outsider, their meetings largely focused around how damaged I was.

I pushed the door open, breathing in the musty, stale smell. It had been empty too long. Carefully and with one hand, I pulled my pants off. Everything took so much longer than before. I slipped the sling off my shoulder, pain immediately shooting through my arm as it was forced to work to hold its position. I placed the collar of my shirt into my mouth, pulling back as I wiggled my non-injured arm free of the sleeve. Then, I used that arm to free the injured one. I stared at my body in the mirror, surprised by how bad my injuries were. I'd never seen them in their entirety. My right shoulder and chest were black and blue, covered by a large, white bandage. The bruise peeked out at every corner of the bandage, not letting me forget it was there. I turned around, looking at the back of my shoulder blade. Unsurprisingly, it didn't look much better, my porcelain skin painted like a canvas of blue, black, purple, green, and yellow.

Unable to look anymore and remain calm, I turned away from the mirror, flipping the faucet on and stepping into the shower without waiting for the icy water to warm. I pulled up the button to turn on the shower as I closed the curtain, jumping out of the way as the still-cool water hit me.

As I felt the water warming, I stepped into the stream, cupping my hand at chin level as the water pooled into my palm. I took a deep breath, unsure whether I was preparing to laugh or cry. I was so incredibly sore that even the slight movement of my shoulders had caused immense pain, but I was stubborn enough to know that I couldn't move at the doctor's recommended pace for recovery. Cole couldn't stay with us for weeks, let alone months, and I needed to be able to take care of myself sooner rather than later.

The truth was, having him in my safe space was terrifying. I'd never allowed myself to grow close to anyone. I'd learned just how easy it was to lose people, and I refused to allow myself to be that vulnerable again.

I moved, wincing as pain shot through me, reminding me of just how vulnerable I was after all. How long could I last like this? How long would I have to? I was beginning to wonder if making it through the anniversary was my first mistake...or if I'd only managed to avoid the inevitable for a little longer. What if they never managed to catch the intruder? What if he came back for me?

Jarring me from my thoughts, I jumped as a fierce knock sounded at the door. I jerked, falling to my knees as intense pain rocketed through me thanks to the sudden movement of my shoulder. I cried out, unable to keep the sound concealed.

"Ellie?" Cassie called, worry in her voice. The door opened, and I saw her shadow through the curtain. I sucked in a haggard breath, attempting to stand as I cradled my hurt shoulder with my good arm. "Are you okay?"

"Mhm," I said a bit too forcefully through the pain. "What is it? What's wrong?"

"The detective is on the phone," she said. "The, um, the one from Fallen Oaks."

As I made it to my feet, I shook my head. "What does he want?" Why would he be calling? Despite the fact that Cole had said Detective McDuffy saved my life, I hadn't seen or heard from him since I woke up in the hospital. Cole said he'd hung around for a while, or so he thought, but we'd never managed to track him down. I'd just assumed he'd given up on us, so what could he possibly want after everything?

"It's…it's about the fingerprints," she said. "The ones on the letter. I think…maybe you should talk to him."

I nodded, though she couldn't see me, and turned off the faucet, reaching for a towel outside of the tub. She placed one in my outstretched arm, and I attempted to toss it over my limp shoulder before leaning out over the tub for the phone. Cassie handed it to me before helping to wrap the towel completely around my body, covering up what I'd missed. I was relieved to hear Cole pacing in the hallway, not daring to come any closer for fear of intruding on what little privacy I had left.

"Hello?"

Thankfully, he wasted no time getting straight to the point. "Ellie, I'm glad to hear you're doing well. It's Detective McDuffy. After the shooting, I was able to get a bit of a rush placed on the fingerprints we were running, and we just got those results back." He lowered his voice just a bit. "Technically, I probably shouldn't be telling you this because we are still investigating what it means, but I wanted you to know…"

"Know what?" I asked, my chest rising and falling with dread.

"Well, the fingerprints came back as a positive match for," he paused, "someone we'd believed to be dead up until this point."

My face contorted with confusion. "What do you mean? Who?" I demanded, pulling the phone from my ear and placing it on speakerphone. There was no way I'd expect Cassie and Cole to believe the news I was going to have to deliver.

"Well, they came back as a match for Dave Thompson. He was a resident of Gerb—"

"I know who he is. I…I don't understand. You *thought* he was dead?" I demanded. "What does that mean? Didn't you find his body?"

The man sighed. "I'm honestly not sure what to make of this. I'm reading through old case files trying to piece things together but it's…it's not clear. The notes are jumbled, and nothing was done like it should've been. The police in Fallen Oaks were understaffed and overworked during the time of your parents' deaths. It doesn't look like Dave had any family to speak of, no one to ask about him. It's not an excuse, even though it sounds like one. I just…I'm trying to get everything figured out off of this paperwork, and it's not clear yet."

"So, what should we do? What are you going to do?"

"I'm working with my team right now to see what we *can* do. We're trying to track Mr. Thompson down, but he's been missing for over five years." He cleared his throat. "I'm sorry, Ellie. I wish I had more to tell you right now, but I don't. I'll be in touch. You guys, er, you be safe, okay?"

"We will," I said softly. "I, um, I never got the chance to say thank you at the hospital for what you did…saving me and all that."

"Don't mention it, kid. No thanks necessary. It's my job."

"Well, thank you anyway," I said firmly.

He seemed as uncomfortable with the entire exchange as I felt. "Okay…well, call if you need anything."

I nodded, not bothering to answer as I heard the line go dead. I looked up at my sister in horror, my bottom lip quivering. The news of what we'd learned sank in like a pillowcase of bricks.

"What do we do?" Cassie asked, her expression equally terrified.

The answer came from down the hall where Cole was still attempting to give me privacy. "We need to warn the others…and Margaret."

We called Monica first, but received no answer. Gray's line also rang until we reached his voicemail. I left them a panicked-sounding message, asking them to call us back in a hurry, and as I hung up from both lines, a sickening feeling washed over me. Neither of them had ever arrived at the hospital, but I'd been so overwhelmed with my recovery and not wanting to pressure them to come after our small fight, I hadn't thought too much about it. Still, I couldn't shake the feeling that I should've asked Cole to call them again between then and now. Before I could dwell on it too much, I looked at Cole, who seemed to have all the answers. He was the only one who could calm the panic in my chest.

"What about Margaret? How do we contact her?" And what if the others never called back? Gray lived in Cincinnati, and Monica was in Arkansas. We'd have to choose one way or the other to head toward, one person over the other.

"We can call the detective," Cole said, after a moment's thought. "Ask him to go check on one of them, and then we can head for the other."

"Or he could just call the local police where they live. They could do a welfare check," I said, the thought occurring to me suddenly.

"Or we could do that ourselves," Cassie said, and I wondered if it was because she still had as strange a feeling about our detective friend as I did.

"But what about Margaret? We can't tell them where she is...even if we knew the address, she said she doesn't want to be found. Her dad is a cop—retired cop—whatever. Disclosing her location could put her in even more danger," Cole said, staring at me as he waited for me to come to the same conclusion he apparently had.

Finally, I nodded, a cold drip of water trailing from my still-wet hair and down my back. I shivered as I answered. "He's right. I hate to say it, but we have to go back."

CHAPTER TWENTY-SEVEN

October 18th

We drove overnight, arriving back in the place I never hoped to see again the next morning. I reached down into the overnight bag from the passenger's seat, grabbing the bottle of pain medicine the doctor had prescribed me and popping another one into my mouth. My muscles and joints were stiff from the car ride, and I was exhausted, having been unable to fall asleep.

Cole looked over, worry written all over his face. "You okay?"

I nodded, taking a sip from the bottle of water he'd placed in the cup holder. I wasn't paying attention to the medicine schedule like I should've been. Every four hours just wasn't cutting it after disobeying the doctor's rules in the shower. I'd spend the next six *years* following his orders if it meant I'd never feel like this again. "Just a little sore," I lied. Cassie was sleeping in the backseat, so we kept our voices low to avoid waking her.

"You're doing a good job with her," he said, seeing me glance back at her in my mirror.

I scowled at him. "Not really."

His head cocked to the side as we turned down the street before we arrived at our old subdivision. "Why do you say that?" he asked.

"Because she's screwed up, Cole. We're all screwed up, and I'm the last person who should be raising a kid." The pills were making me honest if nothing else.

"Then why do you do it?"

"Because I love her," I said plainly. "And no one else would understand what she's gone through like I do."

"You'd do anything to protect her, wouldn't you?"

"Anything at all," I said without having to think about it. There was no question. If my last breath was what would give Cassie twenty more, I'd take it.

"That's what really matters. None of us had someone to protect us that day. Except Cassie. She's always had you, Ellie. No matter what happens, you've protected her from more than you realize. You should remember that."

I narrowed my gaze at him. "What do you mean?"

He shrugged one shoulder, offering up a sad smile. "I just think sometimes you seem really hard on yourself. And I get it…survivor's guilt and all that, but I just thought you should hear someone say you've done a great job." He looked away from me as if something distracted him, but I didn't know what. "You're a really good person, Ellie."

I nearly laughed but managed to contain it. I'd been called a lot of things in my lifetime, but a good person wasn't one of them. I was far from good, and we both knew it. How could any of us be good after all we'd experienced and seen?

"I'm not," I admitted. "But I don't think I'm a bad person either."

"In another life, I think we could've been friends," he told me, and when he looked my way, I noticed a small tear in his eye. Was it the steady flow of cold air from the vent that was causing him to tear up, or something else?

"We've had two lives, Cole, and we weren't really friends in either." As I said it, a tiny bit of hope flickered inside of me that I immediately hated. I didn't want to feel hopeful about Cole. I still wasn't entirely certain of his reasons for helping me, but the one thing I was sure about was that, soon enough, he'd be on his way back to his real life. I couldn't allow myself to care.

When he didn't argue with me, either because he was trying not to argue with the gunshot victim or because what I'd said was true, I leaned my head against the window, letting the conversation come to a natural close. He pulled into the subdivis—er, *park*—easing the car to a stop at the edge of the woods. If I hadn't known it was there, I'd never have seen the path to Margaret's house, but it was easy enough to spot when you knew what you were looking for. He climbed from the car, walking around to my side to open my door. Normally, it was the kind of thing I would've hated, but my arm was too sore to care. Cassie awoke at the lack of rumble from the car and stretched out like a cat. I'd always teased her about that, but I couldn't help finding it cute. Apparently Cole agreed. When I looked over my shoulder at him, he was smiling at her as well.

"Rise and shine, sleepyhead," he whispered, waiting for me to step out of the car before he closed my door and opened hers.

"Should we leave her here?" I asked. "We don't know what we're walking into. What if Mr. Thompson's already here?"

"I'm not staying in the car," Cassie argued.

"I don't think it's safe to leave her either," Cole said at the same time. "Besides, we'll get a good look at the house before we go in. If we see anything suspicious, we can turn around and decide what to do from there."

Cassie climbed from the car without waiting for my permission, shutting the door behind her and staring at me firmly. I was obviously outnumbered, a feeling I was really getting tired of between the two of them, but I sighed and nodded. "Fine, whatever. But if we tell you to get back or to run…"

She saluted me sarcastically. "Aye, aye, captain." I rolled my eyes at her sass, walking around the front of the car and heading straight for the path Margaret had led us down before.

"Let me go first," Cole said, stepping in front of me protectively. We took careful steps across the forest floor, my every sense on high alert. When the house finally came into view, I scanned the horizon, searching for any sign of Margaret or her daughter. To my horror and relief all at once, we didn't see anyone. Cole led us across the yard at a steady pace.

"It doesn't look like she's here," he said as we reached the porch.

"We should at least knock on the door," I said, staring at the small, beveled glass window at the top of the wooden door. "They may just be inside."

He nodded, though his expression clearly said he doubted it. His fist made contact with the wood of the door once, then twice, and he stepped back. His body protected Cassie and me, though it was clear we didn't need protecting—no one was home.

"We should go," I said, suddenly feeling worried. Something wasn't right. Where would they have gone? From what we'd seen of their lives, they seemed to live off the land as much as possible. Though I knew it wasn't entirely impossible that they'd left of their own accord, something in me screamed that that wasn't the case. "We need to contact Detective McDuffy."

"Wait!" Cole called, staring around the back of the house. "Did you hear that?"

I cocked my ear in the direction he was pointing. "Hear what?"

"I heard someone talking," he answered, his voice even lower than before. Why had he said *someone* rather than Margaret? He waved for me to follow him, then pumped his hand up and down as if to say we should move slowly. I nodded, though I could hardly lift my feet with all the fear that suddenly had me rooted to the spot. I wanted to tell Cassie to run since having her there felt less safe than I was comfortable with, but my mouth wasn't working. Cassie passed me, hurrying along after Cole as he grew further ahead of us.

Unfrozen from my trance, I kept my footsteps quiet as I brought up the rear of our train. At least Cassie was tucked safely in between us that way. If something were to happen, one of us could protect her.

The thought was like poison in my brain. I didn't want any of us to need protection again. Hadn't we been through enough? What were we thinking bringing Cassie out into the middle of the danger? We should've left it all for the police. This wasn't our business, and it wasn't our job.

I was mentally scolding myself, trying to find the words and the willpower to convince Cole that we should turn back while we had the chance, when we rounded the corner and Cole turned to face me.

"Ellie, look ou—"

THWACK.

Darkness.

CHAPTER TWENTY-EIGHT

October 19th

Darkness.

Pain.

Wet.

I woke up in a cool puddle of something wet on a hard, concrete surface. My body was stiff, my senses muddled with unfamiliar surroundings. I attempted to sit up, forgetting for a split second about my wound, and whimpered in agony as pain ricocheted through my body.

"Ellie?" I heard her voice, tears of relief forming in my eyes instantly.

"Cassie? Is that you? Are you okay? Where are we? What happened? *Are you okay?*"

She kept her voice low when she answered me. "I'm… okay. We're somewhere inside the house. Margaret hit you on the head with a shovel. Then me. I tried to stop her, but… that's all I remember."

"Cole," I said, remembering that he'd been with us as the

memory of the event flooded back to me. "Cole, are you in here?" I waited for his response, more tears filling my eyes when none came.

"I don't think he's here," Cassie told me, not bothering to elaborate on what that might mean. I couldn't bear to think of the possibilities.

"But where are we? A basement?" It was too wet to be any part of the house that wasn't a basement. At least, I hoped so.

"Maybe," Cassie said quietly. "Are you tied up?"

I rubbed one hand over my damaged arm. "No, I'm not." I paused. "Wait, are you?" I stood, the room around me spinning as I placed a hand on my head, surprised to feel a knot on the left temple. "Ouch."

I heard her sniffling, and I wondered if she was crying or shivering. "Yeah, I am," she said. "My hands."

I wondered why Margaret hadn't bothered to tie me up. The only logical answer being that she hadn't wanted the immense pain it would've caused to my hurt shoulder to wake me up. "Why would Margaret do this?" I wondered out loud, feeling my way around the concrete room in a search to find my sister.

"What do you think she did with Cole?" she asked. I swallowed hard, not wanting to admit all the ways I'd already imagined her killing him. Would she go for the easiest, like a gunshot? Or something more violent, like stabbing? Would he be strong enough to fight her off? Strong enough to save us all?

"I don't know," I said finally. "We're going to get you untied and get out of this room and find out, though."

"Ellie," she whispered frantically as I drew near to her, my hands on her back and then her shoulders. Her body shook with fear and adrenaline.

"It's me," I assured her, moving my good hand down to the ties that bound her to the chair she was sitting in. "It's okay. It's just me."

"No one even knows we're here," she cried, her voice cracking as she said the words. "I don't want to die, Ellie." For the first time in so long, I realized just how young she was. Her voice sounded so childlike, her whimpers filled with too much heartbreak for someone her age. I'd always wanted to protect her, but in that moment, I realized protecting her was no longer just a want, but a need. A piece of the foundation that was who I'd become. If Cassie didn't make it out of there alive, it would only be because I hadn't either.

I leaned down, gripping the rope with my teeth as I attempted to free her with one hand. I tugged until I felt the knot loosening, hoping I wasn't rubbing her skin raw as the rope grew loose around her wrists, and I gave one final tug, freeing her from her binds. She shot up with a gasp, as if her lungs were searching for fresh air, and then I felt her arms around my neck with a hug. She buried her face into my chest, sobs escaping her throat. I smoothed her hair. "Shh, it's okay, Cassie. It's going to be okay. I'm going to get us out of here."

I reached for my back pocket, wondering if they'd discovered my phone. It wasn't there, which was no real surprise to me, but I'd figured it was worth a shot. "There has to be a way out...a room or a basement. Something." I was thinking aloud, walking around the damp room and running my hands along the sweating concrete. Occasionally, I'd stumble over something, but I refused to quit. I had to get us out of there...get to Cole. I had to save us all. This time, I couldn't fail.

The basement was smaller than I'd imagined. I made it around the room and back to Cassie quickly, trying to map out the darkness in my head. There were a few concrete posts in the center of the room and one wooden door on the far side, a room that was sealed with a padlock. Next, I began to search for tools, bending down on my knees and feeling around the floor to no avail.

A noise upstairs alerted me that someone was headed our direction, and I grabbed the first thing I could find, what felt like a long, wooden stick. Perhaps an old broom handle. I felt Cassie move closer to me, though she didn't speak. I would've done anything to protect her. Anything.

Instead, I watched as the door opened, allowing a beam of light to seep into our darkness, and I lowered my weapon as I stared into Cole's face. Then, he lifted the gun.

CHAPTER TWENTY-NINE

October 19th

"Cole, what are you doing?" I asked as I stared down the barrel of an all-too-familiar gun. I stepped in front of Cassie instinctually.

He shook his head, his eyes wet with tears. "I'm sorry," he said. His hand was shaking, and I wondered if he'd ever held a gun before. If he'd ever held *that* gun before. The way he held it looked strange, as if it felt foreign in his hands. "I don't want to do this."

"What are you talking about?" I asked, keeping my voice calmer than I felt. "Why do you have that gun?"

"I never planned to like you, Ellie. Or you, Cassie. I just had to finish the job. That was it, and then I could go home and live my life. Finally."

"What do you mean?" I asked again. Cassie gripped the back of my shirt in her fists, and I heard her trying to stifle sobs. If a bullet was shot in that moment, it would go straight through me and kill us both. There was no doubt. I stepped back, trying to gain some distance between us. "Where's Margaret?"

"She's gone to get Dave," he said. "They'll be back any minute."

"Dave Thompson?" I asked. "He's here?"

"I just said he's not," Cole said angrily. He was obviously agitated, but I still couldn't make my mind put together the pieces.

"Why would she be going to get Dave Thompson?"

"He needs to know it's done," Cole said, switching the gun from one side to the other.

"What's done?" I asked.

"You're dead," he said emotionlessly, though tears were still leaking from his eyes. "Both of you. He needs to know that you're both gone so all of this can stop."

"I don't understand, Cole. I'm...I don't get it." I choked back a sob I hadn't been expecting, my eyes searching the room for a way out. There was nothing. He was blocking our only exit. "Why do we need to die?"

"Because of the curse," he said, his eyes bulging.

"The...curse?" I couldn't believe his words. "What are you talking about, Cole?"

"Ellie, please don't make it harder than it has to be."

"You're...really going to kill us?" I asked, my bottom lip quivering. "Why? I thought you were our friend." It was a childish thing to say, I know, but it's what came out.

"If I don't kill you, the curse continues. I just want it to stop. I just want to live my life in peace. I can't hold down a job, Ellie. I can't make a relationship last. At least you had Cassie." He was already talking about us in the past tense, I realized. A thought that had my stomach in knots. "You weren't alone. I've been alone every day since that morning."

"You aren't alone anymore, though. You have us. You have Monica and Gray."

"Don't you get it?" he demanded. "They're dead. They're all dead. You all have to die in order for it to be over." He rubbed the hand holding the gun across his brow, his forehead slick with sweat. "I didn't make the rules, you know? I just...I have to do it. You'd do the same if you could."

"What are the rules, Cole? Who told you about them?" I asked, taking another step away from him and pushing Cassie with my back.

"Dave did. He told me everything. Made me a deal. If I help him with this, help him kill every relative of the people who bought homes on this land, he'll let me go. Otherwise the deaths will continue. If I ever want to have kids, a wife, I have to do this. Otherwise, I'm putting them at risk too."

"But *you* lived on the land, too, Cole. There has to be another way."

"I wasn't blood," he said, and I did a double take at his words. "I was adopted from foster care when I was six."

"I...had no idea." It was true. I'd never known anything about Cole's past.

"Yeah, apparently the one good thing my shit-mother did was give me her untainted blood. But until the last drop of your blood is spilled, I'm still in danger."

"That doesn't...it doesn't make any sense, Cole. Mr. Thompson lived in Gerbera, too. Why wouldn't he have to die?" I paused, waiting for an answer. He looked down as if trying to figure out if I was making sense but shook his head, so I went on. "Curses aren't real. They can't be. Some curse didn't do this to our families. People did this. Mr. Thompson did. His fingerprints were on the letters. You heard the detective. You don't have to be one of them. You don't have to do this."

"I do, though. I do. I don't have a choice. Do you have any idea what it's like to go from having nothing...living in absolute squalor while your mom shoots up in the bedroom next to yours and bangs some shithead dealer to having everything you could ever want? Parents who cared about you, three meals a day, a future set for me at an Ivy League school, and then to have that taken away before your eyes? All of it... just gone. And then, to top it off, I got put right back in foster care and treated like shit until I aged out of the system. Then, it was right back to minimum wage jobs that I can't even hold because I have so much PTSD from my fucking fucked up past. Seems like I'm right back where I was destined to be all along, doesn't it?" He chuckled maniacally.

"Cole, I can get you help. I can find someone for you to—"

"This," he lifted the gun higher, "is the help I need. When Mr. Thompson contacted me a few weeks ago and told me this was all I had to do to end the curse—track you guys down, give him your addresses, and make sure you died this time—it was a hard decision, Ellie. It was. I never wanted to hurt you guys. In fact, my plan was to warn you and let you run, but tell him you were dead. I tried to find a way to save you, but he saw right through my plan. He wanted to be the one to do it. He had to make sure it was handled. But then he didn't kill you when he shot you, and he said I had to stay with you. I had to get you back here so he could make sure it was done right. When I found out where Margaret lived, he was...really happy with me. Now, they're together again. Happy. And I get to live." He wiped a tear from his eye, distraught. "I don't want to be a bad guy, Ellie. I really don't. I just want to live. That's all I want."

I sucked in a breath, one hand on my stomach as I processed the news. "You…you *planned* this with him? Offered us all up as a sacrifice? Even gave away Margaret's location? How could I have trusted you? How could you do this, Cole?" I felt fat tears blurring my vision, sitting heavy on my lower eyelids. Betrayal. Loss. It was starting to feel like all I'd ever get to experience.

"I had to do it. I'd taken too long to get you here, and then I couldn't get you to stay put long enough for him to make it to Fallen Oaks. Margaret was the only thing I could offer him to make it right. He really does love her, Ellie. He does. And as for your deaths, they were supposed to be painless. I'm not a monster. Just a shot to the head. One and done." He placed his fingers to his temple to imitate a gunshot to the head. "Monica and Gray felt no pain at all. You wouldn't have either, but Cassie distracted Dave for a second." He sighed. "He said she looks so much like Margaret that he hesitated and missed his shot with you. With her brown hair, I don't really see it, but—"

"Monica and G-Gray?" I clutched my chest, stepping back. "They're really…"

"They're gone, Ellie. You two are the only ones stopping the curse from ending now."

I felt bile rising in my throat. "I let you stay in my house. I let you take care of my sister."

"I never planned any of that, honestly. I never planned to stay with you or grow closer to any of you. I've lost enough people. I didn't want to feel this way about losing you. I didn't want to feel anything."

"You don't have to do this. There has to be another way."

Cassie was outright sobbing behind me, and I was beginning to feel lightheaded.

"There is no other way," he said firmly. "Trust me, if there were, I would take it. But this is it… This is my way out. You have to die." He cocked the gun, and I held up a hand, thinking fast.

"Wait! Wait." I shook my head through my tears. "Please."

"I can't," he said. "If I don't do it, he'll kill me, too."

"He'll kill you anyway, Cole. Don't you see that? This was never about the curse. It was about our parents and what they did to Daisy Thompson. The curse was just an excuse for him. He used it as a way to cover up what he'd done."

"No, you're wrong," he said. "He told me it wasn't about that. He's forgiven them."

"Actually, I haven't." The voice boomed from behind Cole, catching us all off guard. Cole spun around just in time to see Dave Thompson lift the gun to his temple. I squeezed my eyes shut, screaming as the gunshot echoed through the basement. I felt Cole's warm blood splatter across my eyes, felt Cassie slide down my legs, her cries the only thing assuring me she was alive and conscious.

I opened my eyes, my stomach immediately seizing as I stared at the mess on the floor. Cole's head lay open on the concrete, brain and blood splattered at my feet. I covered my mouth, throwing up into my palm and watching as the liquid dripped from my hand and slowly mixed together with the blood. I was waiting for my turn. I knew it was coming. I would die just five years and fourteen days after my parents, merely yards from where they had.

I looked up at the man who'd taken everything from me, my eyes narrowing at him. "Haven't you done enough?" I asked, my anger rising.

He looked taken aback by my words. "'Scuse me?" he asked.

"I know you lost your daughter." He raised the gun at my words, but I couldn't stop. I could smell the metallic odor of blood, feel it coating my skin. "And I'm sorry about that. I know it was their fault. But…you've killed so many people."

"Lemme let you in on a secret, Ellie," he said, my name on his lips causing my skin to crawl. He smiled, his yellow teeth showing menacingly. "I like killin' people. I especially like keepin' my promises about killin' people. I promised your parents years ago I'd kill every last person they ever loved. Seems like I'll be keepin' that promise after all, doesn' it?"

I closed my eyes as he raised the gun to my head as he had Cole's. When the shot rang out, I fell to the floor, warm liquid trailing down my leg. I thought it was blood, but after a moment, I realized I smelled urine. I opened one eye and then the other as a hand scooped me up. The shot was ringing in my ear, so it took a moment for his voice to come into focus.

"Detective McDuffy?" I asked too loudly. A team of officers rushed into the small basement, the detective and another officer I didn't recognize removing Cassie and me from the room as quickly as their legs would carry us. I leaned my entire weight on him, unable to carry myself any further. My body shook, my legs like spaghetti, and I felt my stomach churning. I looked back at Cassie, her eyes wide with shock and skin ashen. Her eyes met mine, assuring me that she was alive, though I had no idea what was going on. I'd felt Dave Thompson's body fall next to me, heard the gunshot that had ended his life, but had we just been passed on from one villain to the next? I was beginning to think Cole was right; maybe there was no end to this. Could we trust Detective McDuffy? Could we trust anyone? I stared at the gun in his holster, wondering if I could even trust myself anymore.

Once we were up the stairs and out of the house, the unfamiliar detective eased me onto the grass. "The ambulance is on the way," he promised me, cupping my face in his hands.

Detective McDuffy sat Cassie beside me, looking me over. "Are you hurt? Did he hurt you?"

I shook my head, though that felt like too big of a question to be answering at that moment. "How did you find me? How did you know where we were?"

Surprisingly, he didn't beat around the bush in his answer. "There wasn't enough powder residue left at the scene, and no powder burns on your skin. That was enough to lead me to believe there was a silencer used when you were shot, even though you gave a statement that you remembered the sound. The other detectives weren't so convinced, but we've spoken with your neighbors. No one heard a gunshot. No one except Cole Dennison. Supposedly."

"But I remember the gunshot," I said, shaking my head. I was out of breath, as if I'd been running from the house rather than carried.

Detective McDuffy looked over his shoulder as an ambulance came into view through the woods. It wouldn't be able to make it to us. He looked to his partner and nodded, both of them leaning down to scoop us up. He carried me like a babydoll, my injured arm cradled in my lap while my other was thrown around his shoulder.

"Are you going to explain why Cole and I heard the shot when no one else did?"

"I don't believe you actually heard it. You remember what

Cole told you happened. That's why we don't like victims to speak to anyone before they give their statement. It can be warped. I believe Cole's version of events muddled yours. No one else heard a thing."

I swallowed. Was that possible? Was any of this? "But that doesn't explain how you found us."

"Cole said he came back because he'd heard the gunshot, which was a lie. Once I knew Cole had lied about why he came back to find you, I tried to contact Monica Murphy and Gray McTavish." His eyes studied mine, and I wondered if he was trying to decide if I could handle the news that Cole had already given me.

"They're dead," I said, my eyes trailing down to my stomach as a lump formed in my throat. "Cole told me."

His nod was confirmation of what I'd hoped couldn't be true. "Gunshots. Which meant the only person who hadn't had an attempt on their life, was Cole. And Cassie, of course. I tried to find out more information about him—" He let out a huff. Obviously, my weight was beginning to wear on him, but he continued to trudge along without stopping. "He'd just lost his job. He was past due on rent. It wasn't much, but it was enough to cause suspicion and get a warrant to track his phone. I wanted to see what he was doing. When I saw you here, I ran a property search on the area and found out that it belonged to Melanie Lawrence, Margaret Gold's late mother. I came to find out what you were doing, and I heard the gunshot." We'd reached the ambulance then, and he set me down in the open doors.

"You seem to be good at showing up at just the right time," I told him. "You've saved us both twice."

"I've lost more people than I saved with this one," he said matter-of-factly with a stern expression. "I don't count it as a success. But I'm pleased I could save two. Now, enough chit-chat, let's get you two checked out."

A medic stepped in front of me, her face lit up by a warm smile. "Hi there, I'm Nicole. Do you mind if I take a look at you?"

I shook my head, my throat dry as she pulled back a bit of my hair to look at the gash on my head. She grabbed a packet of gauze, tearing it open and pouring something on it before placing it to my head. "This isn't deep," she said. "That's good." Her eyes narrowed a bit as they met mine. "Do you know what happened?"

"They hit me with a shovel. I was unconscious for…well, I don't know how long."

She pulled the gauze back, looking over the blood-soaked cloth. I hadn't realized I was still bleeding. "I don't think this is all your blood," she told me as she pulled out another piece of gauze and cleaned my face gently. "How's your shoulder?" She stared at the bandage which was now dark crimson, not bothering to touch it right away as she waited for my response. I hadn't realized it was bleeding again, and I wondered what sort of damage I'd done to it.

"Sore," I croaked. She nodded with a sympathetic grimace, reaching out to take my arm and move it slowly.

"I thought so. I need to take the bandage off and see how much you're bleeding, okay? We're going to get you fixed up. It's over now. You're safe." I felt her eyes trailing over me as the last of the blood was wiped from my face and she set to work on my shoulder, moving the limb as carefully as possible. To my left, another medic was tending to Cassie, who appeared to be fine physically, though mentally I knew we were both a wreck. Just in front of us, near the edge of the woods, Detective McDuffy stood next to his partner, their arms folded across their chests. They kept an eye on the clearing, on everything around us, to make sure we were safe.

Suddenly, a car whipped in, its tires squealing on the pavement as it came to a stop in the grass. I turned to look at who it might be, terrified and confused all at once. Had they called my grandmother? Even if they had, I couldn't imagine her rushing over like that.

The driver's side door opened, and a man half-stepped, half-fell from the car. "Margaret?" he cried, his voice carrying through the park. The bald head protruded around the side of the door, and I recognized the tired eyes of Larry Gold. "Did you find her?" he yelled to no one in particular. *"Did you find her?"*

McDuffy stepped up, obviously confused about what was going on. He put a hand up as the former officer attempted to get past him. "I'm sorry, sir. This is a closed crime scene."

"Don't tell me about closed crime scenes. I've been working crime scenes since before you were born. Did you find my daughter?" the man demanded, struggling against the outstretched arm of his replacement.

"Your daughter? Margaret Gold is your daughter?" His jaw dropped, followed quickly by his arm. "You're Lieutenant Gold?"

"Damn right I am. Or, at least, I was." The man straightened his back, sizing up McDuffy. "You're new to the force." It didn't sound like a question, but McDuffy nodded in confirmation.

"Transferred in from Huntington last year."

Gold grumbled. "One of my friends on the force said my Margaret was here. All these years I thought—" His eyes landed on the movement straight ahead. I followed his gaze, ignoring the medic as she continued to see to my shoulder, and saw another officer carrying Millie, with Margaret following close behind, right toward us.

"Margaret! Margaret!" Her father rushed forward, loud sobs escaping his throat as he made it to his daughter through the bramble and brush of the forest. "Oh my God, it's you. All this time I thought I'd never see you again." He grabbed the back of his daughter's neck, squeezing her into a hug. She seemed confused and resistant at first, but finally gave in. I watched her eyes squeeze shut as she hugged him back, though her hug was less enthusiastic. He pulled her away from his chest, looking her over. "My sweet girl…" He choked out the words, his lips pressed together as his face grew red. "I just can't believe it. I looked for you. I looked for you everywhere."

She shook her head, stepping back. "Why didn't you find me?" she asked, a sob escaping her own throat. "Why did you stop looking?"

Her words caused tears to form in my own eyes. I remembered the words she'd said to me, about her father finding her after the murders, about how he'd been responsible for them, and I knew in that moment it couldn't be true. Perhaps those were the things she had to tell herself to survive not being brave enough to contact her family again. Perhaps those were the stories Mr. Thompson had fed her, about how life with her family wouldn't be the same because she was no longer who they wanted. She wasn't the little girl they'd lost. I tossed theories around in my head, but the truth was, she'd lied, I couldn't be sure why. What lies Mr. Thompson had brainwashed her with, I'd never know. But as I stared at Margaret with her father, I felt in my bones that he'd believed she was dead. He hadn't found her…hadn't been able to track her down after she disappeared the second time. There was no way. His sobs were too authentic. If he'd seen her just a few years ago and given up on her, like Margaret had claimed, I didn't believe he would be reacting this way. Then again, I was obviously not the best judge of character.

Interrupting my thoughts, the EMT stepped back into my line of vision. "We need to get you to the hospital," she said. "Just to get your head checked out and make sure you haven't done any further damage to your shoulder. Your wound is open, so it needs to be re-stitched, but I don't think the damage goes beyond that. Let's just get a better look though, okay? I want to make sure. That's a nasty wound you've got there."

I nodded, lying back on the gurney as she gestured for me to do so. Within moments, Cassie was strapped down in the back of the ambulance, too. I reached out to take her hand, my heart rate calming slightly. I looked over at her, rubbing my thumb over her knuckles. "You okay?" I asked.

She swallowed, tears trailing down her cheeks as she gave a half-nod. I knew the truth…that she wasn't okay. That neither of us were okay, and it was likely neither of us would ever be okay again. How was she supposed to say that, though? As I met her eyes, her expression changed. We were together in everything that had happened, and that's what was most important. We'd make it through this like we had everything else. The two of us.

The EMT kept a close eye on us, though I tried to assure her we were fine. She smiled warmly, continuing to check our vitals periodically and wipe the blood from my head as it fell.

My shoulder was throbbing, and I laid my head back on the pillow, my jaw tense as we hit another bump.

"Are you hurting?" Cassie asked.

"I'm okay," I said, shaking my head. I knew she could see through the lie, but she didn't bother to say so.

"We're almost there," the medic said, adjusting in her seat as we slowed down. "I know it doesn't seem like it yet, but you two are really lucky."

I nodded. *Lucky.* Yeah, we'd heard that before.

CHAPTER THIRTY

April 10th
Six Months Later

"Cassie, grab that box," I say, pointing to the last stack of boxes in our apartment. She sighs, wiping sweat from her brow as she lifts it and follows me toward the U-Haul.

We place the last of our belongings inside, and I lift my good arm, pulling the heavy, metal door down with a loud crash. It has been six months since we became the remaining two of the Fallen Oaks Five, and each day things seem to get a little better. I had my last session with Doctor Porter, though he's referred me to a colleague of his once we get to the new city.

I walk toward the apartment, no longer listening for the sounds of someone coming up behind me. I'm not afraid anymore. I don't look for death around every corner or see threats everywhere I go.

Since the deaths, the truth has come out about everything. Margaret told the police how Mr. Thompson had convinced her that her father had given up searching for her and how, when he'd disappeared, she'd believed her father had killed him and the rest of Gerbera. She was angry with her father, which was why she'd disappeared to her mother's dilapidated house after she'd escaped the room during the massacres. Mr. Thompson hadn't been able to track her down until Cole gave away her location, at which point Mr. Thompson swore to her that if she helped him carry out his final act of revenge, he would leave her and Millie, his daughter, alone for good.

Margaret and I have grown close in the months since the events of the anniversary. She often reaches out to me for help with certain details as she works out the kinks of her new memoir. The biggest revelation she will reveal in her book is the fact that Mr. Thompson had managed to stir up the sympathy and fear of some of the townspeople in order to complete his mission. So much so that they'd been willing to help him commit the murders of innocent people. All to save themselves from a nonexistent curse. I guess it's true what they say: people will do anything to save themselves, no matter who else may get hurt in the process.

Margaret believes most of the police thought her father was involved in the massacre, which was why it wasn't investigated as it should've been, though Lieutenant Gold actually had nothing to do with any of it.

It was only when Detective McDuffy took over, unaware of the reasons not to dig into our case, that some of the truth was revealed.

I'm not sure how to feel about our parents anymore, whether or not they were more or less guilty than Mr.

Thompson. They were reckless, and they'd cost an innocent child her life. Can I ever forgive them for that? Sometimes when I look back, I feel hatred for all we went through because of them. Sometimes it's grief for all we've lost. Other times, I think of all the good they did afterward. Did they spend their lives trying to repent for what they'd done? Had they somehow made up for it? Is there a penance for such a sin?

Cassie asks me those questions a lot, and I try my best to answer them. Our parents made mistakes. But, then again, the undeniable truth is that we all made mistakes. Cole. Mr. Thompson. Margaret. We were all a part of the web brought on by one mistake. One decision.

We have to live with that and move on; that is all that's left. When we relocate to Seattle, we'll start over once again —something we are growing pretty good at, except this time it will feel like an actual restart.

I've spoken to Detective McDuffy, Margaret, and our grandmother to let them know that we'll be leaving, but I didn't bother to say where we'd go. I don't think I want them to know. Cassie and I deserve to be invisible somewhere. We deserve to have our freedom for the first time in our lives. Freedom from what we've been through. Freedom from what we've done.

I think this will be my last journal entry for a while. Possibly forever. Time to pack the journals away and start living my life. Doctor Porter isn't sure it's a great idea, but I'll talk to the new therapist and see.

I think back sometimes, about all we've been through, and I wonder if maybe we were lucky in some ways after all. In the end, we get a fresh start at a whole new life. We get to do whatever we choose. Isn't having the choice to do whatever you want with your life the best gift anyone could give you?

I hope so. It's what I gave her.

CHAPTER THIRTY-ONE

Margaret,

I hope this letter finds you well. I'm sure you've heard by now of my sister's passing. It was very sudden, and I'm still at a loss for where to go or what to do next. I know you two had grown very close, and since you are one of the few who knows about everything that happened, I thought I could trust you with something that is concerning me. I trust I'll have your discretion with this.

I was sorting through her apartment recently, and I came upon this journal with a pretty detailed description of everything that happened when we came back to Fallen Oaks the last time. She had a box full of journals, most of which have nothing to do with those events, but if you'd like to take a look at the rest, just let me know. Postage is expensive, so I will save that until I know you're interested.

I'm also including a printed out email that I found in the box. It was sent to her work email address and I suspect it's from Dave Thompson. I was pretty shocked to find this, because Ellie never mentioned having received it, but it seems like Dave may have offered Ellie the same deal he offered Cole—hand over the rest of the Fallen Oaks Five in exchange for him letting the two of us survive. There's no indication on the email of whether or not she took the deal (I want to believe she couldn't have, right?), so I wondered if she'd ever mentioned anything about it to you?

It's not like her to keep something like that from me...

Also, this has me wondering if Gray and Monica were offered the same deal, and if so, if he offered the deal to each of them, which ones—besides Cole—took it. It's almost like he got some sick pleasure out of torturing us, since it doesn't seem like he intended to actually let any of us live. As for how he found any of us, I still don't know, but my guess is that he had some connection in the police department. I know you mentioned that suspicion in your book, and I find more and more that it makes sense.

Anyway, I'm including that email as well as a photo of her before she started her chemo. She wanted me to have it to remember her how she was, and I think she'd like for you and Millie to do the same.

My sister was a quiet person who didn't like to let anyone close to her, but I know she cared about you. I know the contact you two have had over the past ten years has really meant the world to her, and I'd like to thank you for being there for her in ways that I couldn't.

I especially like her last journal entry. She seemed hopeful. I never saw that side of her. She was always the cynic, but it makes me happy (well, less sad anyway) to think of her as having hope. She knew Seattle would bring us so much good, and I truly believe it has.

Despite it all, a recurring theme in the journals was how much she would do to protect me and to give me a better life, and she did. She saved me, Margaret. She gave me a future. I've thought about this long and hard, trying to decide if I could ever forgive her if I learned that she had taken the deal like Cole did, and the truth is, I think I could forgive her for anything. I see how much she sacrificed. This journal gave me that.

I really got to know my sister through her journals, and I hope that they will give you some peace as well. If you ever need to talk, you can reach out. Please let me know what you think about the email when you get a chance.

All the best,

Cassie Delanoe

Ellie,

We're back and we're coming for you all.

The choice is yours...

Turn in Cole Dennison, Gray McTavish, and Monica Murphy, and I will spare you and your sister's lives.

You have three days to decide. Collect the addresses and await further instructions.

Happy Anniversary.

DON'T MISS THE NEXT DOMESTIC THRILLER FROM KIERSTEN MODGLIN!

They had the perfect marriage until the cracks began to show. Who is lying in this twisted domestic suspense? Better question: who isn't?

Read *I Said Yes* today:
https://amzn.to/30XX1gv

DON'T MISS THE NEXT KIERSTEN MODGLIN RELEASE!

Thank you so much for reading this story. I'd love to invite you to sign up for my mailing list and text alerts so we can be sure you don't miss my next release.

Sign up for my mailing list here:
http://eepurl.com/dhiRRv
Sign up for my text alerts here:
www.kierstenmodglinauthor.com/textalerts.html

ENJOYED THE LUCKY ONES?

If you enjoyed this story, please consider leaving me a quick review. It doesn't have to be long—just a few words will do. Who knows? Your review might be the thing that encourages a future reader to take a chance on my work!

To leave a review, please visit:
https://amzn.to/2QIhS30

Check out *The Lucky Ones* on Goodreads:
http://bit.ly/2sFjqCB

ACKNOWLEDGMENTS

I'm so incredibly *lucky* to have an amazing group of people in my corner.

To my husband, Michael, and my sweet daughter, CB: thank you for loving me. Thank you for never getting too upset when my answer to your question is "Just a second, let me finish this sentence before I forget it" and for being my biggest support system.

To my family, Mom, Dad, Granny, Papa, Nan, Pop, Kaitie, Kortnee, Kyleigh, Uncle Tommy, Aunt Velma, Aunt Lori, Aunt Judy, and the rest of our big bunch: thank you for always being there for me, cheering for my victories and listening when I fail. Thank you for giving me the strength to believe in myself and chase this crazy dream.

To my Twisted Readers: thank you guys for believing in every single story I put in front of you. Thank you for cheering me on and for always, always loving my characters like I do. I couldn't do this without you.

To my 4 Authors and a Mystery sisters, Emerald O'Brien, Laurén Lee, and Rachel Renee: what would I do without you ladies? I'm so incredibly grateful for every single conversation we have and for the amazing friendship we've found in each other. You all inspire me to do better and be better every day. Love you!

To my editor, Sarah West: thank you for always seeing the story I'm trying to tell within the mess that I hand you. I'm incredibly lucky to have found an editor who truly gets my characters like you do.

To my proofreaders, the amazing team at My Brother's Editor: thank you for polishing this book until it shone. I'm so grateful to work with you.

And lastly, to my fans, my loyal readers: thank you for all you do to support me and my art. Thank you for believing in me, purchasing my stories, sharing them with friends, reviewing them online, and so much more. Without you, none of this would be possible.

ABOUT THE AUTHOR

Kiersten Modglin is an Amazon Top 30 bestselling author of psychological thrillers, a member of International Thriller Writers and the Alliance of Independent Authors, a KDP Select All-Star, and a ThrillerFix Best Psychological Thriller Award Recipient. Kiersten grew up in rural Western Kentucky with dreams of someday publishing a book or two. With more than twenty-five books published to date, Kiersten now lives in Nashville, Tennessee with her husband, daughter, and their two Boston Terriers: Cedric and Georgie. She is best known for her unpredictable psychological suspense. Kiersten's work is currently being translated into multiple languages and readers across the world refer to her as 'The Queen of Twists.' A Netflix addict, Shonda Rhimes super-fan, psychology fanatic, and indoor enthusiast, Kiersten enjoys rainy days spent with her nose in a book.

Sign up for Kiersten's newsletter here:
http://eepurl.com/b3cNFP
Sign up for text alerts from Kiersten here:

www.kierstenmodglinauthor.com/textalerts.html

www.kierstenmodglinauthor.com
www.facebook.com/kierstenmodglinauthor
www.facebook.com/groups/kmodsquad
www.twitter.com/kmodglinauthor
www.instagram.com/kierstenmodglinauthor
www.tiktok.com/@kierstenmodglinauthor
www.goodreads.com/kierstenmodglinauthor
www.bookbub.com/authors/kiersten-modglin
www.amazon.com/author/kierstenmodglin

ALSO BY KIERSTEN MODGLIN

STANDALONE NOVELS

Becoming Mrs. Abbott

The List

The Missing Piece

Playing Jenna

The Beginning After

The Good Neighbors

The Better Choice

I Said Yes

The Mother-in-Law

The Dream Job

The Liar's Wife

My Husband's Secret

The Perfect Getaway

The Arrangement

The Roommate

The Missing

Just Married

Our Little Secret

Missing Daughter

The Reunion

THE MESSES SERIES

The Cleaner (The Messes, #1)

The Healer (The Messes, #2)

The Liar (The Messes, #3)

The Prisoner (The Messes, #4)

NOVELLAS

The Long Route: A Lover's Landing Novella

The Stranger in the Woods: A Crimson Falls Novella

THE LOCKE INDUSTRIES NOVELS

The Nanny's Secret

www.ingramcontent.com/pod-product-compliance
Lightning Source LLC
Chambersburg PA
CBHW030608310726
48979CB00003B/621

* 9 7 8 1 9 5 6 5 3 8 1 4 4 *